"Don't that major by the Gatling bear a striking resemblance to ole Torn Slater?"

Suddenly all fifty Rangers were going for their guns and at the same instant Slater was diving off his mount, straight for the Gatling. He reached the crank, just as the first Rangers cleared their guns. Instantly he had the handle turning, going directly for the greatest concentration of Rangers, the ones clogging the center of the street. The psychological effect of that 1500 round-per-minute buzzsaw, ripping through their ranks, was shattering.

If they had refused to give way before, they yielded the road now . . .

Novels by
JACKSON CAIN

Hellbreak Country

Savage Blood

Hangman's Whip

Hell Hound

Devil's Sting*

Published by
WARNER BOOKS

*Coming soon

JACKSON CAIN

WARNER BOOKS

A Warner Communications Company

WARNER BOOKS EDITION

Copyright © 1984 by Jackson Cain
All rights reserved.

Warner Books, Inc.
666 Fifth Avenue
New York, N.Y. 10103

 A Warner Communications Company

Printed in the United States of America

First Printing: October, 1984

10 9 8 7 6 5 4 3 2 1

Special thanks to
Les Kreyer, Steve Keen, Dave Moscow and Fred Walski
and to
Dana Ludington and Charlie P.
*for helping me out on Jake Logan and for taking a stand on
Jackson Cain*

Thanks again to
Bruce Brill, John Nelson and Wayne Zirkle
for making me feel at home in Little Rock

And, last but not least,
Robert Guerrieri
my real-life model for Outlaw Torn Slater

I am indebted to Robert Gleason and John Kelly for permission to quote from their songs, "Calamity," "Yuma Jail," and "Beware of the Bear" on pp. 219–222, 281 and 283–85. Their work had provided the basic text for J.P. Paxton's "The Ballad of Outlaw Torn Slater" and has been a constant inspiration to me throughout the writing of these books.

Cry "Havoc!" and let slip the dogs of war.
—*Julius Caesar*, III, i, 273

PART I

1

A big black dog with a huge head, a wolfish muzzle, and the massive chest of a yearling steer swaggered through the Comanchero camp. His dreamy eyes were heavy lidded and half-asleep. He was known to all the renegades as Bear Dog.

The reason for the name was glaringly apparent. He was five feet from the tip of his nose to the end of his rump, and he stood four feet shoulder-high. He had black hair and powerful shoulders, so he did not look like an average dog but something fiercer, larger, more formidable.

Except for the wolf's mask, he looked more bearlike than canine.

Then came the walk. As he lumbered through the camp, he was clearly the boss dog. No beast offered him challenge. Even the most foolishly brave gave Bear Dog trail.

He had been challenged in the past. The camp's toughest animals—its shepherds, Alsatians, its one pit bull, its biggest mutts—all had tried their luck. The results were predictable. The settlement animals mistook Bear Dog for one of their own and fought him as such—a fellow hound to be sniffed and studied, snarled at with bristling, stiff-legged menace, and then, after a long ritualized dance of low-throated growls and bared teeth, taken on. Finally, when one of them whimpered and whined, flattened to the ground in a gesture of surrender, the fight would come to its harmless close.

But Bear Dog never learned this battle etiquette. The offspring of a mastiff and a bitch-wolf, raised in the wild by a murderous wolf pack, Bear Dog knew no rules. Kill or be killed. Eat or be eaten. That was all. When challenged, his muzzle corrugated from the tip of his nose to the tops of his eyes in a horrific, feral snarl. His mane bristled in waves, ears pressed tightly against his head; his eyes gleamed hatefully; his lips pulled back taut against his teeth; his fangs flashed and dripped slaver. He never learned the rules of the camp. He never learned to play, to tease, or even to threaten. He only knew the way of the trail. To hit and to hit hard, shoulder to shoulder. Using his superior weight and strength as a battering ram, he knocked the other dogs off their feet. Then, while his opponents lay helpless, he went for the jugular. Driving his fangs deep into their necks, he tore open their throats. Blood drenching his muzzle and chest, his fur rising up and down the length of his coat, he would rear back on his haunches. His throat would spasm in a bone-chilling wail. The other dogs would flatten around him in abject submission, then whimper and whine.

And Bear Dog reigned supreme.

So he made his rounds, lumbering sleepily through the Comanchero camp, blinking his heavy-lidded eyes, policing the area. It was near dusk. The camp was awash in a pale ghostly glow, the desert sky crimson streaked. In the camp everything seemed in abeyance, lost and immobile in the shimmering desert heat, in the endless veil of amber dust and the deepening twilight gloom.

On and on Bear Dog walked. His snout seemed to wrinkle in a frown. Occasionally, at twilight, when all was quiet, an uncomfortable emptiness settled over him. In truth, he did not like the ways of the camp. Often he felt lost in a maze of unclassifiable smells. The odors of men and their possessions, their women, and their emotions swept over him in chaotic layers. Their smells, it seemed to him, were filled with contradictory emotions, with sadness and pain, with sex and death.

But there was meat in the camp, while often on the desert trails none existed. And he had a leader here who was strong, who was to be respected, followed, and obeyed. He had possessions to guard, dogs to fight, and bitches to mount.

Still, it was not his way.

His was the meat trail in the lands to the north where there was game aplenty—quail to flush, track lines to run, bucks to pull down. The way of the camp, especially in the quiet of dusk, often seemed to him a damming up of his life's wild tide, a thwarting of his strongest desires. In the still hush of the overpopulated settlement lay only emptiness and dim incomprehension.

Other things baffled him. The way men loved to tie things up. The way they hung their still-warm meat from trees, posts, and racks, then pegged out the raw wet hides. The way they tied up the young dogs when they sought to teach them subservience, duty, and the meaning of the whip.

Even stranger was the way they tied up each other. Earlier in the day, a man had been roped by his neck and genitals to a buckboard and dragged up and down the camp till he was little more than a side of raw bleeding meat. The men, white and Indian alike, had laughed. Those in the freight-wagon brothels and bucksaw shacks had risen with their whores and walked to the doorways, pointed their fingers at the bloody man, inverted their whiskey jugs, and had not lowered them till they were sucking air. When the man was at death's door, they had staked him out like one of the endless green hides pegged all over the camp.

Then they had spread-eagled this man beside a hill of fire ants.

Soon his body was a virtual mountain of angry red ants, which frantically devoured his eyes, mouth, and genitals in a bloody frenzy because wild honey had been smeared over those parts.

Now only a few men stood by and watched.

The rest slept in shacks and tents, snoring loudly, drunkenly.

Bear Dog raised his eyes from the spread-eagled man. Just beyond him, a pure-blooded Apache was suspended by the thumbs from the hanging rack. The man's eyes were rolled back till only the whites showed. His mouth moved noiselessly, though every other part of his body was motionless, paralyzed with pain.

Bear Dog recognized this man's people. The Indian was from a tribe with whom Bear Dog had once lived. He knew them by their broad short bodies, thick chests, and massive heads. Their hair was black as ravens' wings, often twisted and woven into thick braids. He recognized these Apaches as brave men who cringed at nothing. Even when scared shitless, sweatless, and pissless, torn limb from limb like plucked chickens, they refused to whimper or submit.

Of course, their being tortured, instead of simply and efficiently killed, made no sense. The fact that Bear Dog's leader had the strength, the power, and the will to do these things was apparently all that mattered. That was why Bear Dog toiled in his leader's service. That was why the Apache agonized in silence.

The leaders did things because they could do them, pure and simple.

And those who served, suffered.

2

Inside the bucksaw brothel shack, three men huddled in the dim light of a coal-oil lamp. They sat on empty Arbuckle's boxes. The bar consisted of raw planks spread across old whiskey barrels along the rear wall. Around the floor, a half-dozen outlaws slumbered beside several half-naked camp doxies. But these three, unable to sleep, sat and talked.

The big one, Lorenzo, was a half-blood Comanche. Hawk-faced, his skin was sandpapered a rough red brown by the harsh desert sun and his own Caddo blood. His frayed plainsman's shirt and his battered tan hat were bleached a colorless gray by the desert sun.

He was staring down the bar at the *Mejicano mestizo compadre* wearing dirty white peon garb, a scoop-brimmed sombrero of filthy, sweat-stained felt, and crisscrossed bandoleers. Most of the canvas loops were empty.

He glared contemptuously at the gringo named Packer, who was wearing the same colorless plainsman's clothes as himself. Packer grinned back at him, his smile filled with malice and broken teeth. Then Packer looked down at his feet and stopped smiling. He had lost his boots in a card game and was reduced to rope sandals.

In the warped mirror of Packer's face, Lorenzo feared that he saw himself. Lorenzo grumbled under his breath, "That bastard Slater. What's Flynn doin' saddlin' us with him? Think we be babies or something? Need Torn-fuckin'-Slater to wipe our noses for us?"

"*Es verdad,*" the Mex said amiably and reached for Lorenzo's jug of mescal.

Lorenzo's wrist quirt with the shot-loaded butt and the double-plaited lash sang across the bar and whipped three tight loops around the Mex's wrist.

"*No, verdad?*" the Mex asked, still agreeable.

"*No fuckin' verdad,*" said Lorenzo.

The door swung open and a big rawboned man in a black slouch hat and a fringed buckskin shirt walked in. His face was hard, angular, heavily lined. He kept a Winchester in his right hand, its butt braced on his hip. Without looking at Lorenzo, he went straight to the bottle, jerked out the cork with his teeth, and spat it across the room. He nodded toward the men on the floor.

"Them boys look stone fuckin' dead."

"Stone fuckin' drunk, you mean."

"Never knew a man yet could hold his liquor like a bottle." He took another big pull from Lorenzo's jug.

Lorenzo stared a hard minute at his bottle. "You push, Carver. You really push."

Carver belched, then fixed Lorenzo with a

tight stare. "What's this I hear you saying 'bout not needin' Torn Slater?"

"Just that. Ain't there already too many of us splittin' the take after Flynn and Flaco get done hoggin' their half? Goddammit anyway, he's old. He can't hack it no more."

"You gonna tell Slater that?"

"Yeah. Maybe play a tune on his head while I do it," Lorenzo said.

"You gotta have *muchos cojones* to fuck around with Torn Slater. Most people think of Slater, their *cojones* shrink right into their stomachs."

"Shit. I'll take that bastard down just like that." Lorenzo snapped his fingers and grinned, his eyes unnaturally bright. "Maybe bend him over the plank bar, pull his pockets out. Shove my Colt into his mouth, say: 'Git up the money, punk.'" His grin was crooked and twitching.

"Who do you think Slater is?" Carver asked incredulously.

"He fucks with me, he's just another asshole 'bout to die."

"Yeah, you real tough. You a bon-ee-fide no-shit bandido, huh, Lorenzo?"

"You sayin' I can't do it?"

"No, just sayin' it ain't been done before."

"That's bullshit, 'less'n nobody had the balls to try."

Carver looked away, shaking his head.

"That be the case, I bet," Lorenzo said. "Ain't nobody had the balls to throw down on him."

Carver shook his head wearily. "You rock on, boy, they all dead."

"Just like he's gonna be."

"You want my advice, give him room."

"Why? What can it cost me?"

"Your good reputation."

The room exploded with derisive laughter, which made Lorenzo even angrier.

"You tell Slater he best watch out for his own reputation. All he'll get from me's a reputation for bein' dead."

Carver stared at Lorenzo long and hard. Slowly, contemptuously, he shook his head, then grabbed the bottle and took a long pull.

"Yeah?" Lorenzo sneered. "Then just listen to this. Come morning, you see me walkin' 'round this camp my pockets stuffed with pesos, what you think then?"

Carver snorted. "How you gonna get it?"

"I'll get it. I got something the entire camp'll want a piece of."

"You gonna have a mighty sore asshole gettin' butt-fucked by the whole damn camp," Packer said, snorting.

Everyone convulsed with laughter.

But then Carver's eyes narrowed. "Okay, Lorenzo. I'll bite. Where you think you gonna get all them pesos?"

"My dog." There. He had let it out.

"We're gonna pay Lorenzo to fuck a dog?" Packer asked, puzzled.

Carver shook his head. "He's too big. Damn dog'd fuck *him*."

After the laughter subsided, Lorenzo shouted angrily, "Ain't nobody fuckin' the dog. We're gonna pit him."

"What you gonna pit him against?" Carver

asked. "He's killed pretty near every hound in the camp."

"Oh, I'll pit him."

"Why should anyone put up their money?" Carver asked.

"'Cause they're gonna see what I'm pittin' him against. I'll let them fuckers trap and pit a javelina. Like the one you trapped in the dead-fall down by the gorge last spring. A fuckin' javelina! Hell, the camp'll give us odds."

"So'll I," Carver said. "Them wild boars, hell, they'll gut a dog from throat to balls."

"S'pose I told you them javelinas ain't that tough? I put one down just last week. It weighed in at a good eighty, ninety pounds, and it weren't shit."

"That was a Sharps 'Big Fifty' you smoked him with. From fifty yards away."

"Guess again." Lorenzo reached under the bar and pulled a recently tanned javelina hide out from behind the whiskey barrel. "Take a look."

They drew closer. In the anterior neck portion of the hide were three round holes.

"What are those?"

"Bear Dog's teeth, you assholes."

"What?"

"I didn't kill him with no 'Big Fifty.' Bear Dog killed him. I was there. I saw it all. He killed him square. Head to head. That big boar javelina didn't have a chance."

"Damn, that dog is *bad*." Carver whistled appreciatively.

"Bad enough to make us a fortune," Lorenzo agreed.

Carver nodded.

"With you two playing the shill, I can whip out half the camp."

"And split it with Flynn?"

"Fuck Flynn."

"That haired-over hardcase? He's too damn tough to fuck."

"I'll do it."

"And what about Slater?"

"Flynn's got to get him out first," Lorenzo said. "He's still in that jail."

"If Flynn can't do it, nobody can."

"Assumin' they both ain't hanged by a lynch mob."

"That mob done tried to lynch him twice." Lorenzo grunted, pointing to a newspaper that one of the half-naked whores was using for a blanket.

"That be the truth, sport, that it be," said Carver. He handed the half-empty mescal jug back to Lorenzo.

PART II

3

Slater paced slowly in his one-window, one-man cell and listened to the mob just outside the wall. He sat on the mattressless bench that served as his bed. He placed his hands on his knees and shut his eyes.

Here he was—thirty-six years old and fading fast. His sweat-rotted, collarless shirt and torn, dirt-caked Levi's attested to that. As did his battered, down-at-the heels boots. As did his heavily scarred body: torso slashed diagonally, groin to shoulder, by an ancient Yankee bayonet; the puckered bullet holes where the bullet had entered below the right side of the clavicle and exited just above the shoulder blade; the broad white whip welts of Yuma and Sonora prisons striping his back.

There wasn't much to show for twenty years on the owlhoot. Some big scores here and there, all quickly spent on high-stakes poker, brothel doxies, and pilgrim whiskey. A few big blowouts in places like San Francisco, Denver, and Saint Louis, but most of the time just fucking off in cow towns and mining camps, places with names like Hayes and Deadwood and Abilene. A few friends were left on his backtrail, men like Hickok, Bill Cody, and Cochise. But the rest of them, high-line riders like himself, were either dead or doing time, and the world was better for it. Men like Frank and Jess, Coleman Younger, his blood-brother Geronimo, and kill-crazed free-booters like Quantrill and Bloody Bill. And he thought of others, too—many, no doubt, good men whom he'd left dead or maimed or broken in spirit, victims of his raiding-party youth with the Apaches, the blue-bellies he'd slaughtered at Shiloh, the red-legging corpses he'd left behind in Bloody Kansas, the sum and spirit and sub-stance of twenty years on the outlaw trail.

A life not spent but a life misspent.

He looked up from the floor and saw a padre standing outside his cell. The priest was big, a good six-foot-three, with a luxurious downward-sweeping mustache and a full beard. His shoulder-length hair was pulled back into braids. His nose had been broken more than once, and though his teeth shone brilliantly, his grin never reached his eyes.

Nor should it have.

This was no man of the cloth.

If he were a priest, Slater was a cloistered nun.

He was looking at Gentleman Jim Flynn.

Comanchero.

Flynn turned to the two guards behind him. He paused a moment as if to study them. One deputy was wearing a broadcloth shirt, brown canvas pants, and a flat-brimmed, flat-crowned plainsman's hat. The other favored a white linen shirt, a black frock coat, and a black bowler. Their badges were brightly polished.

For a moment Flynn said nothing. Then he cleared his throat. "May I have a few minutes alone with the prisoner? It is customary. The law states that all condemned men must have a few moments to consider the worth of their immortal souls."

"I know," Bowler Hat said with a sneer, "but this here's a bad 'un. Get too close to the bars, you'll think you been dragged through a pepper mill dick-first."

Gentleman Flynn gave them his most ingratiating smile. "Please, constables, I am hardly a novice in these matters, having once served as Judge Parker's chaplain. And anyway, given the state of that mob out there, I think Mr. Slater will be a little hesitant about working them up any further. If he hopes to survive the night. Now if you will, a little privacy, please?"

"Your funeral, padre," said Bowler Hat. As the two went back into the office, he cracked, "Never held with mackeral snappers."

"Bible-beating bullshit artists what they are," agreed the other.

When they were alone, Flynn's grin brightened a few more candlepower. This time it reached his eyes. "Outlaw Torn Slater. I thought you were the stud duck around here."

"Do I look it?"

"You sure do," Flynn said, raking Slater up and down with a mocking glance. After taking in the filthy clothes, he met Slater's eyes. "You'll have to tell me your tailor."

"Fuck you, Flynn."

"Temper, temper, my boy." Flynn surveyed the six other cages, four empty, two containing passed-out, dead-drunk Mexican drovers. "My God, what a hole. How's the food?"

"Tastes like horse bran."

"Oh, come now, it can't be that bad. After all, for a man of your machismo, what are a few inconveniences?"

"Yeah, I know. Hardship improves the character."

"My friend, a long jump, a short rope, and a taut noose are the only things that will improve your character."

"That ain't very *padre*like of you."

The grin widened. "You mean you're afraid of dying?"

"I ain't 'fraid of nothing 'cept low cards, bad whiskey, and honest women."

"That's the attitude, sport. I so admire bravery and laughter in the face of death."

Slater pointed to the Good Book tucked under Flynn's arm. "Tell me, that Bible good for anything?"

"Sure."

Flynn opened it and tore out half a page. Putting the Bible back under his arm, he took out a bag of Bull Durham and rolled a smoke. He twisted the ends, licked the quirly, and stuck it in his mouth.

Slater averted his eyes and gazed around his

cell glumly. "You know, some days it just don't pay to duck."

Flynn passed the quirly between the bars to Slater. "You must buck up, good man. In the Holy Mother Church the only irredeemable sin is hopelessness."

"Naw, I got shut of that hope shit years ago. Anymore, I just live for the day."

"In that case, sport, I doubt this day will be one of your all-time greats."

An empty whiskey bottle came crashing through the small barred window high up on the cell's wall.

"Ah, me," Flynn said, merry as a gravedigger, "a small *mémento-mori* from your lynch-crazed admirers."

"Them mementos come in here with fair regularity." Slater pointed to the scattering of shards and slivers across his cell floor.

"Let's see the note," said Flynn, pointing to the folded paper lying amid the broken glass.

Slater picked it up and handed it to Flynn through the bars.

Flynn read it aloud: "'We got you by the balls, son of a bitch. Now we start to pull.' Ah, the man is a poet at heart. Do you sense his feeling for language? The cadence? The imagery?"

"Flynn, what do you want?"

"I want you to think of me as a friend. No, as a sort of father confessor."

"You'll be a priest the day Christ comes back and dies of syphilis."

"Yes, distinctions do blur. Anymore it's hard to tell the Christians from the lions, isn't it?"

"So what do you want from me?"

"Faith. The faith of a little child."

"And?"

"And the hundred fifty thousand you so maliciously absconded with from the Brownsville Guarantee and Trust."

"You mean you want me to tell you where it's hid, right between these here bars?"

"In good faith."

"What's your share?"

"One hundred and fifty thou'."

"That's hard."

"So's hanging."

Another bottle came crashing through the barred window. This one was filled with piss. Some of it splattered on Flynn's pants leg.

"Motherfucker!" he shouted, incensed.

The door burst open, and Bowler Hat shoved his head in. He stared dubiously at Flynn. "What was that I heard?"

Flynn flashed him his broadest, sweetest smile. "A sacred prayer of the Holy Mother Church. Now, my good sir, another moment please. Our friend was just finishing a sincere act of contrition."

The door shut. Except for the drunken derelicts, they were alone. Flynn removed a small hip flask and helped himself to a snort. He offered one to Slater. "A little alcohol to purify the palate?"

Slater took a swig and returned it.

"I still say the price is high."

"So are your windy dreams of freedom."

"Yeah? What would I do with all that freedom anyway?" Slater said, pointing beyond the walls.

"You'd find women to fuck, lawmen to kill, trains to rob. The usual."

"I still say it's hard."

"Harder than an eight-minute egg. But then, you have no choice. You're down to your last stack of blues. So just push them across the table, my boy. Time to bet blind."

Another bottle crashed through the barred window, but neither of them looked.

"Skates like mighty thin ice."

"Oh, we'll make it all right. With a little luck and no lame ponies. Yes, we'll make it."

"How?"

"Even as we speak, men are tunneling under this rear wall from the empty building next door. They will plant a dynamite charge beneath that wall. When it goes, it will disperse the lynch mob, remove half this jailhouse, and, assuming you don't die in the blast, free your sorry soul."

"Suppose I say no?"

"Then stand by that wall."

"Suppose I don't want to."

"Then I'll recommend that the deputies draw bull's-eyes on your ass. That way, after the hanging, schoolboys can chuck rocks."

"Flynn, you're one hard *hombre*."

"My enemies say I cause plagues, famine, and earthquakes."

"You're harder than that."

"Only in the heart."

"That blast could kill a lot of innocent men."

"There's no such thing as an innocent man."

"And what if this thing don't work?"

"Your name shall be entered in Foxe's *Book of Martyrs*."

"Shit."

Just then the outer door opened.

The deputies entered. Flynn looked dejected. He said to Slater, "I'd hoped, my son, I'd brought you something to believe in."

"Like pussy, tequila, and fists full of pesos?"

"I feel as though I've lost."

"You did. So do it gracefully. Get the fuck out."

As Flynn turned toward the door, the deputies were grinning. Flynn looked back at Slater. "God is not a graceful loser."

Slater pointed at Flynn's mustache. "Maybe His priests'd do better if they shaved off them wimpy-lookin' poon brooms."

The two deps exploded in hilarity, and Flynn made his exit.

4

Underneath the jailhouse, two timbermen braced the hastily dug tunnel wall. They were small, squirrelly men, their clothes and bodies black with grime, faces shiny with sweat and fright. In the weird glow of the guttering candle, their eyes were huge as saucers.

On they worked. Above them, the pine planks that they'd spread over the upright two-by-fours buckled and groaned. Dust coughed out of the ceiling chinks and cracks with each nerve-grating creak, blinding, gagging, and terrifying them.

So they worked like hell, shoring up the shaft.

Torrez, the lead timberman, called to his partner, "It's his fault." He hunched lower in the three-by-three-foot shaft and drove another two-by-four up alongside the wall, then topped it and its mate with a pine plank, hammering it between the ceiling and the tops of the joists.

"Yeah?" the grizzled old man at the front of the tunnel yelled back.

"Damn straight," Torrez said. "You been bending and weaving this fucking drift all over hell's creation. We ain't got enough shoring timber for a tunnel half this size, and now that we finally get under the jail wall, you make us stop and wait."

"Ever hear of rock, you stupid lunkheads? We been running into it ever since we dug out of that basement. Big outcrops of bedrock, three spires in all. Course we been detouring around them. What did you expect me to do? Eat my way through all that granite?"

"Yeah? Well, we're here now, ain't we?" the second timberman cracked.

The old man held his *Deutsch Uhr* stem-winder up to the candle. "Yes, and by the looks of this fine old Bremerhaven railroad watch, we still have two more minutes. Those are Flynn's orders."

"But we can't keep the ceiling up that long," Torrez shouted.

The old man cackled gleefully, indifferent to their fear. "Ah, my feather-headed friends, you should have seen me in '48 in the California fields. Or Virginia City. Or the Comstock. Me and the boys I mined with, hell, we'd called a simple dig like this a cakewalk. Talk about dog-mean drudgery, talk about pain and terror and dying, talk of cave-ins and rock falls, talk of drifting and shafting, dreaming and scheming on them long-dead, back-country main lodes, hell, you boys should have seen the Yukon in '53."

"I'm getting out of here," Torrez shouted.

"You're fucking A," his partner said.

"The old bastard's lost his goddamn mind," Torrez said, turning in his tracks and heading back down the tunnel.

Then they heard it. At first it was a faint rumble, a sort of low, deep-throated growl, followed by tiny bursts of black smoky dust billowing down into the shaft. Then the volume of the rumble increased till it sounded more like the muted roar of a distant locomotive far, far down a tunnel. The chugging and pounding grew, then, till it was one continuous, hair-raising howl, a din of almost ear-splitting intensity, like the crazed screams of a hydrophobic wolf pack gone mad with feral suffering. The tunnel was pitch black with the smoky influx of dust and debris, and it seemed that every inch of the shaft was simultaneously coming apart at the seams.

By now the roar was elemental, almost skull-cracking, as the now-invisible timbers buckled and bowed, screaming like tormented souls in hell under the incredible strain of the cave-in. The world was collapsing all about them as they choked and gasped in the dense clouds of inky dust.

For a long moment Torrez lay crushed and almost asphyxiated by the cave-in. Then he suddenly felt himself being jerked out of the surprisingly shallow shaft by a crowd of two dozen men. After he wiped the dirt from his eyes, he saw that his friends had made it too.

There they were, just like himself, rubbing their dirt-blackened eyes.

Surrounded by the shouting, riotous mob.

For a moment the crowd seemed leaderless. Individual voices were heard shouting:

"They was trying to tunnel Slater out. They was part of his gang."

"String 'em up!"

"Three more for the sycamore!"

"Hang the bastards high!"

Finally a big, bearded man in a white linen shirt, a black bowler, and a matching frock coat waved his hands for silence.

"Come, gentlemen, we are not barbarians. First these men get a fair trial."

"And then we swing 'em!" someone howled in the background.

"Perhaps," the bearded man said, "but first a

few questions. Were they digging a tunnel under the jail?"

"*Yes!*"

"Is Outlaw Torn Slater residing therein?"

"*Yes!*"

"Were they, then, attempting to get Slater into that tunnel?"

"*Yes!*"

"Do we turn them over to some lily-livered, pussyfooting, weak-kneed, bleeding-heart eastern judge who'll slap 'em on the wrists and let them go?"

"*No!*"

"So what do we do?"

"*Telegraph 'em home!*"

"*Trim the fuckin' trees!*"

"*Ride 'em under cottonwoods!*"

"*Dress 'em in hemp!*"

"*Three more for the sycamore!*"

"*Swing 'em!*"

"*Swing 'em!*"

"*Swing 'em!*"

Once more the leader raised his hands for quiet, this time his face a contorted mask of horror. Suddenly there was quiet for real—dead quiet. Quiet save for the soft sputtering that came from the remains of the up-tunnel shaft, just beneath the jailhouse wall.

Accompanying the faint buzz was the acrid fragrance of burning cordite.

"Fuse smoke!" someone shouted.

The three sappers were the farthest from the jailhouse.

Which was what saved them.

That plus the fact that the crowd shielded them from the impact.

Because then it went! With a thunderous *ka-whomp! Whomp! Whomp!*

A red-orange fireball rose above the tar-black mushroom cloud of smoke, the blazing detonation containing not only the jailhouse wall but the brains, bones, and blood of two dozen erstwhile vigilantes.

When all the debris settled, it was as if the jail's rear wall had never been.

5

Gentleman Jim Flynn, still wearing his cassock, retreated into the deputies' office just as the cry of "Fuse smoke!" sounded. At that instant, Slater threw himself to the floor directly alongside the bars on the far side of his cell, hauling the wood bench on top of him.

The blast all but knocked him out. When it was over, he found himself staring at the vanished wall and the smoky, starlit world beyond.

Suddenly, miraculously, he was free.

He scrambled to his feet.

"Hold it there, partner. Don't move. Don't even blink."

"Or you're dead fucking meat."

He didn't have to turn to identify the voices. The two deps. They'd been in their office when the blast hit. They had been quicker recovering since they were farther from the explosion.

They were standing directly outside the cell door.

It would not do to leave this mortal coil shot from behind. The men who carved his scallop could do it to his face.

He turned.

Later it would occur to him that he had shown extraordinary self-control. He did not twitch, grin, or blink. His face was immovable as death throughout it all.

Even at the sight of Flynn sneaking back into the jailhouse.

Flynn was pulling a stagged-off hand-grip Greener out of his baggy pants. The scattergun was no more than ten inches long, from its chopped-down stock to its sawed-off double-barreled tip. Flynn raised and aimed it, elbows locked, arms extended.

The sight of Flynn should have been enough to betray emotion in any mortal man.

But not Slater.

As the deps glared at Slater over their Colts, Bowler Hat said to him, "In fact, you're dead meat anyway."

Flynn cocked the sawed-off, the clicks unmistakable, startlingly loud. One barrel, Slater knew, would be loaded with cayenne pepper and birdshot; the other with lye and number-two goose. It was a recipe Satan had cooked up special and patented for himself.

It was Flynn's standard load.

Flynn let go. The room filled with a blinding cloud of black-powder smoke. Slater choked on the acrid fumes, his face scorched and blackened by the blast.

But anything he felt couldn't match the spectacle in front of him.

The two deps were blown face-first into the bars, both fists clutching them, faces jammed against the cage, the cayenne and lye searing their ripped, blood-streaming backs.

They stared at Slater in agonized surprise. Slowly their grips on the bars slackened, and they slid down the iron struts, faces still pressed against the cage, first Bowler Hat, then the other.

Instantly, Slater had their two Colts in his belt, and Flynn had cut the bloody key ring off Bowler Hat's belt. The door was open, starlight winking through the smoking, crumbled wall, and Flynn and Slater were through the hole, guns drawn, while a band of Comancheros just outside the demolished jailhouse held their waiting mounts.

PART III

6

Bear Dog waited outside the brothel shack, beside the doorway, his muzzle resting on his crossed paws. He looked up with expressionless eyes as his Lorenzo walked out of the whorehouse. Lorenzo squinted against the glaring morning light, then stared across the compound at the sporting pit.

Bear Dog turned his head. He'd been aware of the activity over there all morning. Two dozen Comancheros with crisscrossed bandoleers and battered sombreros surrounded the pit. They knelt, wagering and shouting.

Lorenzo struck out across the camp and Bear Dog fell in beside him.

Over the past year Bear Dog had come to see Lorenzo not only as a new pack leader but as a source of food. The ways in which Lorenzo got their meat were bizarre beyond comprehension, but still, through Lorenzo he did eat. And in this harsh, barren desert country, a constant supply of food and water was all that counted.

Nonetheless, Lorenzo's methods for meat gathering were baffling. Take the rituals of the pit.

Lorenzo must have pitted Bear Dog fifty times over the last year. Into the pit went Bear Dog and his foe. Week after week, month after month.

Thus, as Bear crossed the camp with its smoking cook fires, its canvas-walled saloons and buck-saw brothel shacks, he felt no fear. He'd been there before. He'd killed, and he would kill again. It was the way of this new and puzzling meat trail.

Lorenzo had no reason for anxiety either. He had something unique in Bear Dog, something his friends had not yet fathomed. Since the dog followed Lorenzo as a leader, they thought him just another mutt bartered from an Apache for a box of shells and a jug of Injun whiskey. Of course, he was bigger, stronger, and tougher than the other hounds, and was a superlative protector of Lorenzo's person and possessions. But that was all. To the Comanchero camp, he was just a dog.

They could not know his origins. They could not know that this dog had survived in the wild. He had lived among wolf packs and along the high lines. Bear Dog had spent years of his life wandering the rimrock on the single-o. He knew the ways of men and had lived among both the Apache and the white-eyes. For when the terrain was too rough and dry, the game and water scarce, he needed men to survive.

But when there was game aplenty, and bucks to pull down and waterholes to prowl, he left these men as simply and abruptly as he had joined them.

He survived. On Bear Dog's backtrail lay the

bones of more dead animals than a man could imagine. Deer, badgers, otter, raccoons, squirrels, fowl and fish of every description, porcupines, antelope, pronghorns, jackrabbits, and even a moose. With wolf packs he'd pulled down bison and pumas.

So it was part of Lorenzo's shrewdness that he had intuited in Bear not only strength and cunning but a savagery that transcended either bloodlust or pride. Bear Dog, very simply, could get it done. His killing instincts were those of the wolf; his intelligence was that of the dog. His imagination in combat tactics rivaled that of man.

Furthermore, Lorenzo grasped something else in Bear Dog, something that lay close to his own bloody Comanchero soul. He was not only elusive as smoke and powerful as a locomotive. In battle Bear Dog lost himself. He rose above the limits of the flesh and found himself heedless and free, close to the wild beating heart of life.

So they walked toward the pit without apprehension. The sleepy-eyed hound who cared for neither creature nor man, and the man who cared only for women, whiskey, and shiny double eagles.

7

It was at the pit that Bear Dog discovered something was wrong.

In fact, everything was wrong. The shouted curses of the crowd were too loud. The stench of their liquor and their sweat and the oily metallic smell of their guns were oppressive. Suddenly, when he was shoved into the narrow gorge, tumbling twenty feet straight down, he knew he was in for it.

At first he lay there in the bottom of the deep hole, his belly flattened against the hard-packed earth. The fall had temporarily knocked the wind out of him, and he needed time to size up the situation.

He did not have long to wait. From above he heard the crack of the ancient two-wheeled oxcart, and he knew something was coming. Closer and closer the cart creaked, and gradually the musky scent of its occupant drifted into the pit. Bear Dog's hackles stiffened. His muzzle lifted, ears flattened against his head, and a growl throbbed deep in his throat, coursing out of him in a flood. It towered to a crescendo, held for a long horrible moment, then soared maddeningly, more wail than roar. Big-time trouble was coming to meet the Bear.

Javelina.

He'd fought them before. The tusked desert pigs were among the most ferocious beasts on the continent, and he'd always come out bloodied and scarred. One time, in fact, he'd taken on three at the same time, and though he'd killed them all, he had been hideously gored.

But in his other battles with javelinas there had been a difference. He had fought them in the open, and his bulk, speed, and quick intelligence had given him the edge. He'd slammed them shoulder to shoulder, stunned and pinned them. Though he'd always been hurt, eventually they had died.

But not this one.

He recognized the pig by his scent and instantly understood the danger. This was not an ordinary javelina, the sort that roamed the American and Mexican deserts in small tight families, and that attacked only when the group was menaced. No; he'd seen, smelled, and trailed this one countless times. This one was a big boar monster of a javelina, a bizarre mutant over four feet long, standing three feet shoulder-high and weighing two hundred pounds.

Even Lorenzo was upset. Bear Dog could hear his leader's voice over the din of the mob. Bear Dog did not understand the words, but from the tone the meaning was clear.

"You scum-sucking sons of bitches," Lorenzo

shouted. "I've been tricked. That ain't no pig. That thing's a bull bison."

"Ey, fuck you, man. You said you'd pit him against a wild pig. So Chucho found one. You put the money down, my friend. You play, you pay."

"Fuck you, greaser."

"And you too, you gringo *hideputa*. Where you shit and where you eat."

Bear Dog ignored the arguments.

Instead, he listened in horror to the straining creak of the two-wheeled oxcart. When he looked up, he saw it tipping on its axle. The wagon bed was open along the jump, and as Bear Dog watched, petrified, the pig's cage careened down the tilted cart.

The javelina thrashed madly inside.

The cage slid out over the jump and into the pit. Just below the rim it snapped to a hard, sudden stop, where it swayed slowly from a taut rope. A second line—a loose pull rope—was tied off along the top of the dead-fall, where it hung looped and slack.

In the pit the sick-sweet stench of the boar javelina was overwhelming. Bear Dog's muzzle writhed and corrugated from the tops of his eyes to the tip of his nose, and his bared teeth were slathered with foam. His ears were laid back flat against his skull, and the deep bass growl once more rumbled far down in his throat, surging through him like a banshee howl from the abyss, soaring insanely, reverberating through the pit as if all the echo chambers in hell were thundering simultaneously.

The cage continued its swaying, maddening descent, swinging from one side of the closed off arroyo wall to the other. The sleepy, dreamy-eyed dog was now a raging red-eyed fiend—lips curled and snarling, fangs flashing, eyes blazing—and the monstrous javelina was evil incarnate. Four feet long, three feet high, it matched Bear Dog pound for pound. From each side of the elongated head, the deeply set crimson eyes burned down into him like balefire. On each side of the cylindrical snout—flat on the end with wide snorting nostrils—were two downward-curving tusks, each a full foot long. The skin was heavy and thick, covered with coarse bristles, the tail long and tufted.

The beast looked to be nothing but bristles, hooves, and tusks.

By now the box was halfway down the pit, and the boar javelina was trumpeting his rage. Great long echoing blasts of *ow-eeee! ow-eeee! ow-eeee!* thundered up and down the abyss, merging with Bear Dog's mad feral wails.

Then it happened. Five feet from the bottom of the pit, as Bear Dog leaped and snapped, spun and growled, the line on the dead-fall's top grew taut and jerked.

Like a shot, the wild pig was out of the cage.

Instantly, Bear Dog flanked the boar and struck.

It was a good hit. He caught the big swine on the side of the upper throat, tearing off half an ear, driving his fangs deep into the bristle-covered neck. Then, getting his legs underneath him and tightening his purchase on the beast, Bear

Dog used all his strength to drive the pig across the floor, slamming him into the side wall.

Blood fountained all over the pit. Had Bear Dog managed to drive his way under the pig's bristly throat, he might have ripped open the jugular, but the howling swine found his own footing. The boar flattened his throat and belly tight against the hard-packed earth, and the friction of the heavy underside dragging along the rough ground braked hard against the dog's drive. Bear Dog failed to turn him over for the throat-slashing kill.

The javelina spun away from the wall, simultaneously lowering his head, and driving up the downward-curving tusks, and Bear Dog felt the sudden rip of the arching fangs. He somersaulted away from the wall, still clinging to the pig but with the curved tusks driving up under his exposed throat. The hunter was the hunted. Bear Dog felt the boar again driving up underneath him, and instantly he let go, retreating across the pit to rethink his strategy.

The beasts circled each other warily. Each had felt the other's fangs, and the pit was wet with their gore.

Bear Dog was the more agile, and he danced in and out, dodging and feinting like a prizefighter. With each bob and weave he struck, taking back a bloody trophy. Here he ripped open the snout. There he slashed the pig's slitted eyes. The flanks and shoulders were raked with gory fang marks.

But the boar javelina was old and wise. He kept low to the ground with unvarying patience.

Gradually, the memory of the slashing tusks faded and Bear Dog grew more confident. His lip curled in a grotesque similacrum of a grin, and he approached the wild boar stiff-legged, menacing, tail up. The bloody map of scars on the boar's body inflamed his feral arrogance, and he strutted cockily.

At last, Bear Dog was ready.

He heaved back on his haunches—forelegs rigid as ramrods, neck fur stiffening, teeth bared, fangs flashing.

And he charged.

But when the dog launched his attack, the pig—eyeing him calmly, unblinking—was prepared. He ducked the wild leap and drove the downward-arching tusks deep into Bear Dog's right flank.

Then he rammed the dog like a locomotive.

The retaliatory charge caught the hound by surprise, and for the first time in his pit-fighting life, Bear Dog was rolled onto his back by an adversary. The pig bore down on Bear Dog's underbelly, driving in to disembowel him. Bear felt the pull of panic and rolled rapidly away from the slashing blades, hysterical with rage.

Unfortunately, the pig could charge faster than Bear Dog could roll, and the boar was on him in a flash. Instantly he was standing stiff-legged over the dog's throat, the tusks descending for the kill. All cunning and imagination gone, Bear Dog was simply a mindless fighting machine, driven mad by the desire to survive.

It was this insane passion that saved him.

Seizing on the closest piece of the pig he

could find, he clamped his jaws on him as hard as he knew how, not knowing or caring what he had.

A split second before the tusks were to slash the Bear's throat, the javelina collapsed. Bear spun to his right, then rolled over on top of the big boar.

His jaws were still locked around the shattered femur.

The wild pig was hopelessly crippled, in unbearable agony, and lying helplessly on his back.

He bellowed, *"Ow-eeee! Ow-eeee! Ow-eeee!"*

The javelina never made it to the fourth roar.

Bear Dog's lunge for the exposed throat was stunningly swift.

With one slashing rip, the animal's life's blood flooded the pit.

PART IV

8

It was two days and nights before the Comanchero band threw off the posse. By then they were only a week's ride from their fortified mountain camp. They felt it safe to picket the ponies, put out a watch, and cook some grub.

While the sentries covered their backtrail and the others ate and slept, Flynn and Slater hunkered down by the cook fire and talked. Over a shared bottle of Old Crow, Slater gestured toward the sleeping Comancheros. His eyes were hard with contempt.

"Imagine," Slater said, "riding with men who sell guns, whiskey, and white women to Comanches. Traveling with the worst Mexican, mestizo, and half-breed scum in the entire border country, men who are not simply outlaws but traitors to two countries. Coman-fucking-cheros. Flynn, why the hell do you do it?"

"The usual reasons: futures, stock options, the lavish pension plan, all my accumulated vacation pay and sick-time."

Slater shook his head sadly. "Pretty sleazy

work for a man of your dignity. White slavery too? Fairly fucking disgusting."

Flynn's grin was wicked. "Fairly fucking lucrative, you mean." Slater looked pained, which seemed to brighten Flynn's spirits. "Come on, boyo, buck up," he said. "Oh, I know you must think me insensitive. You know, lacking a conscience? A moral code?"

"Something like that."

"Well, I've pondered that wanted poster of yours, too. Seen the latest version? My God, they have you down for everything from stealing apples to killing Christ. There must be sixty, seventy capital offenses under your name. And that bottom line, 'Wanted: Dead.' Apparently taking you alive is no longer a viable alternative. Tell me, what kind of man gets a dodger like that? Judas Iscariot?"

"You got a point," Slater said unenthusiastically. "Anyway, I s'pose I owe you a thank-you for getting me out of the hoosegow."

"No thanks necessary. I'll be remunerated."

"Still, it took guts blasting me out of that jailhouse."

"So? A sow's got guts. Two hundred and eighty pounds of them. She's still a pig."

"Damn, Flynn, you're one hard rock."

"Saltier than a summer lick."

Slater glanced disdainfully at the two dozen slovenly outlaws rolled up in their sougans. "You sure you know what you're doin'?"

"If I did, I wouldn't be fucking with these Comancheros."

"I be your witness there."

Flynn fixed him with a tight stare. "You sure you know where that bank money is? Papers say it was never found. One hundred and fifty thousand dollars vanished into smoke."

"Oh, it's around."

The stare turned harder, the eyes flat now. "Don't fuck with me, Slater."

"Really?"

"Not till I'm dead and cremated, with a stake driven through my ashes."

"Why?"

"'Cause I'm too much like you. We're brothers of the same black bloody bowel. We both come from the same dark hell."

"You mean you crawled out from under the same slimy rock?"

The crack came not from Slater but a mestizo renegade named Flaco. He was a big swarthy Mexican with nut-brown skin, a hooked nose, a hawk face, and a downward-sweeping bandido mustache. His chest was crisscrossed by heavy bandoleers, their canvas webbing with brass-rimmed cartridges gleaming in the firelight. Flaco grinned crookedly.

His nickname was "Bloody" Flaco.

"Flaco here is my segundo, my second-in-command," Flynn explained, ignoring the gibe.

"Who's number three?" Slater asked.

"Name's Lorenzo."

"Who's he?"

"*Uno hombre duro*—a hard man," said Flynn. "You may have some trouble with him."

"How much trouble?"

"He's a real haired-over hardcase," Flynn said.

"Likes to pull his bullshit gun-punk number quite a bit, like he was Bill Hickok or something."

Slater rubbed his nose. "Is he Bill Hickok?"

"What he is," Flaco said, "is about a hundred eighty pounds of condemned pork. In a ninety-pound bag. A big tricked-out saddle on a fifteen-dollar horse. I think he just learned that women don't have cocks."

"I asked if he was tough."

"He's got a lotta hard bark on him."

"Smart?"

"He thinks he's real deep."

"You care if I kill him?"

Flaco started laughing. "You shoot him, the shit'll run out so fast, all'll be left is skin and bones."

"I mean is he your friend?" Slater asked Flynn.

"I got no friends."

Flaco started laughing again, but Flynn's face was deadly serious. "You ignore this fool," he said, nodding toward Flaco. "He can laugh all he wants, but Lorenzo's holed his share. Give him a step, you're a dead man."

"Why the speech?"

"We got no one to bodyguard you, and right now you're worth something to us."

Slater rubbed his crotch. "What are the women like in your camp? Pretty? I ain't had a woman in over two months."

Again Flaco laughed.

"What's so funny?"

Flynn stared at him meditatively. "It'd be like the Medusa jumped out of her cave and gave you head."

"Who's the Medusa?"

"Let's just say she was not one of your all-time lookers," said Flynn.

Slater felt Flaco watching him. Slater returned the look. "Am I s'posed to say something?"

"Yeah, amigo, like where you stashed them pesos."

"Not subtle but direct. I like that, Flaco," Flynn said.

Slater nodded his agreement. "Where are the pesos? That's easy, partner. The same place they've always been. The Brownsville Guarantee and Trust."

Flynn's face was grim. "My friend, I never joke about money."

"Who's jokin'?"

Flaco's face was also grave.

"I also recommended that you never fuck with me," Flynn said.

Slater met the hard stare coolly. "Flynn, you may be hell with a drop-forged blue-steel hard-on, mean enough to kill a rock. But that don't change the facts. That money's still in the Brownsville bank. In fact, it never fuckin' left."

"What?"

"The one-fifty belonged to Diaz and a limey tycoon named Sutherland. Got word it was there from an inside source. What I didn't know was that the inside source was playin' both ends against the middle, and when I made the score, them bags, 'stead of bein' filled with double eagles, was packed mostly with washers. The coins was just on the top."

"Why wasn't this in the papers?" Flaco asked skeptically.

"The limey dude, Sutherland, covered it up. The fucker's smarter'n a sheep-killin' dog. He had his deposit insured with Lloyd's of London, so he filed a claim and got his half back in insurance money. As well as keeping his and Diaz's share."

Flaco whistled softly. "Man fuck with Diaz, he gotta have *muchos cojones*. Most men even think of the don, their *cojones* retreat right up their assholes."

"You're shucking us, friend." Flynn's voice was not pleasant.

"You mean the truth hurts?"

"No, I mean you do not understand. I am not a graceful loser. I react badly to business reversals. I mean you have to do better. Much better. The Brownsville bank will not do, not after all the blood, sweat, and expense we've gone to springing you from that jail."

"I never asked for your help."

"But you took it. Meaning you are not out of the cane. Meaning we play by certain rules here. The rules are relentlessly harsh."

"Meaning?"

"Meaning you hit that lode till your hammer breaks. In short, you come up with that one-fifty."

"Or?"

"Or you die where you stand. Slow and hard."

For a long moment Slater studied Flaco and Flynn. He figured he had a good chance of gunning them both, before the others got to him, though Flaco looked like more than a fair hand. Even so, he would never outgun the other Comancheros. There was no future in throwing down on these two.

Slater let it out slowly. "Then it's for the hammer. We go where the money is, just like you want."

"How?" Flynn's voice was incredulous.

"We take the Brownsville bank."

9

For a long time they stared at each other across the fire.

"I ain't sayin' it'll be simple," Slater finally said.

"Ain't simple?" Flaco half-shouted. "It ain't even sane."

Flynn's voice was calm but equally skeptical. "My friend, when you talk Brownsville you are talking blue-bellies as well as Pinkertons. Ever since you hit that establishment twice in five months, once reputedly for the one-fifty, that bank has been under constant federal protection."

"And I say it can be taken."

"Maybe by the Army of Virginia, led by Bobby Lee and Old Stonewall. But not us."

"Look, I have a friend."

"He better be Ulysses Simpson Grant."

"No, but he's a man who can get anything, do anything. I say the bank can be had."

"Okay, say all that's true. I hear they now got one of them fancy locks on the safe. The kind that can't be busted open by force."

"Then we go to the bank president. We reason with him."

"Reason with him?"

"Yeah, I shove my Colt in his mouth, ease back the hammer, and say, 'Okay, hoss, where's them fuckin' pesos?'"

"I hear the vault's time-locked."

"I hear different."

"You're going to look mighty foolish we go in there and can't get the safe open."

"Like a baby pig caught nursin' on the stud boar. But I still say it can be done."

"I don't feature it."

"Look, I got this friend. Immanual Carpenter. He runs guns and ammunition and anything military. He's a *revolucionario*, a *Contra-Diaziste. Muerta a Diaz*,"—death to Diaz—"it's his whole life. He hears we're hitting a bank where Diaz has stashed his currency, he'll find us a way into that vault."

Flynn shook his head gloomily. "Damn, I hate the idea of getting shot to death in broad daylight on the Brownsville streets."

"Not us, amigos," Slater said.

"Yeah?"

"Diamondbacks don't die short of sundown."

"And there's no place like home, and no friend like Jesus," said Flynn.

Slater grinned. "Next you'll tell me love is eternal."

"Not if it gets your dick in a doorjamb."

"Yeah? Well, the hardtail fact is this bank can still be taken."

"Square deal?" Flaco asked, his eyes dubious.

"Square as a plumb bob."

"I still say you're shucking yourself around. You're looking for roses where the cactus dies."

"Naw, I just hear a different drummer."

"He must be playing a death march."

"It can be done."

Flaco stared at Flynn a long minute. "He's harder to discourage'n a snake-oil salesman."

Gentleman Jim Flynn merely shook his head. "No, he sees this as a passport to paradise. And who knows, maybe it is."

"If I was free as a bird," Flaco said, "I wouldn't go for anything as crazy as this."

"Ah, hell, why the fuck not?" Flynn said morosely. "We've already been convicted of murder, mayhem, and white slavery. May as well be charged with being fools."

"The blue-bellies, the Pinks, the Texas Rangers, the Brownsville law. If we pull this off, they'll come down on us like a falling building."

"Indeed. 'Cry Havoc! and let slip the dogs of war,'" Flynn orated.

"What's that?" Flaco asked.

"Literature, amigo. You wouldn't understand."

"It means he's been reading Buntline's novels again," Flaco said.

"And stealing all his best lines," said Slater.

"It's gonna be hell, you realize?" Flaco said to Flynn.

"With a busted cinch."

It was Slater's turn to grin. "Now that that's settled, anything else I should know about this Lorenzo fucker?"

"Yeah. Don't pet his puppy."

"What kind of degenerates are you?" Slater asked, contorting his face in mock disgust.

"No, I mean his dog. The man's got himself this hound, see? Half-mastiff, half-timber wolf. Nothin' but teeth, hair, and hard-ons. You can probably gun Lorenzo no sweat, but that dog is bigger'n Beelzebub and mean enough to kill Jesus. I'd get the dog first."

"I don't know. I was always partial to dogs."

"Try and remember that when he's dragging your intestines out your asshole," said Flaco. "This is no ordinary hound."

"Do more than remember," Flynn said. "We're talking hell hound. Hits like a hydraulic hose. You can kill Lorenzo if you want, but you best blast the hound first. Otherwise you're deader'n Abe Lincoln's nuts."

PART V

10

Bear Dog was in the pit again.

It had been ten days since the fight with the javelina, and once more he knew something was wrong. Most of all, the men up top bothered him. The two dozen Comancheros and his pack leader, Lorenzo, were always cause for concern. But now he had another man to worry about: the strange-looking, duded-up gent in the muttonchop whiskers, black frock coat, floral-pattern brocade vest, and black stovepipe hat.

Clearly, something ominous was happening. This time there was no screaming and cursing.

The men spoke in hushed tones.

The sleepy-looking dog with the massive black body, the huge head, and the look of perpetual boredom glanced topside.

Things were quiet up there.

Too quiet.

11

Up top, the center of attention was the dandy in the frock coat and the stovepipe hat. Joshua T. Whitfield, circus performer extraordinaire.

"You mean to tell me," Lorenzo said to the frock-coated man with the muttonchops, "that you are absolutely, one-hundred-percent convinced that no dog can whip that thousand-pound grizzly of yours?"

"Sir, as I have been explaining half the night, and most of the day," Whitfield said, helping himself once more from his shiny silver flask, "*Ursus horribilis,* otherwise known to you gentlemen as the grizzly bear, can and will whip any *canis* that has ever lifted a leg to piss. I do admit that yonder griz, presently caged on that wagon, is not your usual run of *Ursus.* Tiny is a bona fide artist, a master of the minuet, a veritable prince of the ballet, a—"

"Easy over, professor. Ain't nobody here come to see him dance. We be here to watch him fight. You say this big bear, Tiny, can't be brought to bay by no mortal dog? Well, maybe we got just the hell hound to get it done."

"Impossible."

Lorenzo shrugged. "How many here side with the professor?"

Eighteen Comancheros shouted their approval.

Lorenzo looked around at his three friends. "That leaves just little ol' me to cover all these bets. Well, I still be flush from the javelina fight. I figure I can do her. Chucho, why don't you start takin' up that action."

Lorenzo turned to Joshua Whitfield. "Professor, go get your bear."

Those with money to wager flocked around Chucho. The rest followed Joshua T. Whitfield, who sauntered toward his caged bear. As Whitfield and the mob rounded the rise, they passed another man walking toward Lorenzo.

Carver.

"Well?" said Lorenzo.

"I don't know," said Carver.

"What do you mean?" Lorenzo said.

"I gave him the meat. It was full of ground glass, lye, diamondback venom, the whole mix. He gobbled it up like it was son-of-a-bitch stew, belched, and went to sleep."

"And no one saw you?"

"Who cares? All of us been throwin' scraps to that silver-tip."

"Did he look sick?"

"No. In fact, Tiny looked kind of satisfied, contentedlike. More than anything he looked sleepy."

"Carver, this better work."

"Don't 'Carver' me. It wasn't my idea to pit that damn dog against no bait-poisoned bear."

Lorenzo nodded grimly. "Yeah, but I still say

it'll work. No mortal beast could take that much internal punishment and stand up to Bear Dog."

"You sure?"

"Yeah, I'm sure."

"Good."

"Why's it good?"

" 'Cause I just seen that bear. He's sleeping like a fucking baby. But you so damned sure, then I say great."

Carver started walking away. Lorenzo grabbed his arm. "Where you going?"

"To get some of that action off Chucho."

12

Bear Dog was hysterical by the time the two spans of mules were lowering the grizzly's steel-barred cage into the pit. No one had to tell him what was in that box.

His muzzle corrugated. The fur bristled in waves up and down his back and across his withers. His tail stood straight up, and his ears laid flush against his skull. Foam frothed insanely from his bared fangs, and he circled the bottom of the pit in a crazed frenzy as he howled.

Tiny was not in much better shape. He was roaring as though all the legions of hell were in him fighting to get out. Once again, the pit thundered like an ear-cracking echo chamber.

Slowly, creakingly, an inch at a time, the cage made its descent.

Compounding Bear Dog's rage was the memory of his first experience with *Ursus horribilis*. He was only a pup running with a wolf pack in the high-plains country. His mother had been a bitch-wolf, his father a pure-blooded mastiff. The pack—forty of them in all—had bayed a grizzly against a giant oak. When the attack was over, twenty-seven of the full-grown wolves lay dead around the tree, as well as his own mother and his mastiff father. The rest of them, sorely battered, slashed, and dazed, beat a dispirited retreat, like the walking wounded of a routed army thudding its long death march home.

Now Bear Dog faced another silver-tip.

In the pit.

And this griz was also in a black rage. Bear Dog could tell. As the huge beast hunkered down on his surprisingly short legs, he was clearly deranged by pain. All one thousand pounds of him—from the tip of his nose to his humped withers and down his silvery spine to the end of his stumpy tail—every square inch of him was in agony.

This was not a good sign. *Ursus horribilis* in his gentlest moods was possessed by a strength and ferocity of astonishing proportions. But when in pain, he became almost supernatural in his strength and fury.

Bear Dog knew this well. He'd studied the claw marks of the old boar grizzlies on hardwood trees, and had always been impressed by the power that had scored that wood so high and deep. In his cub days, after he had seen that first griz decimate his pack, he'd come between a sow griz and her den and witnessed the placid berry-feeding creature explode into the devil's own cattle prod. She had come howling out of that wood straight for him like a roaring, smoking locomotive. Bear Dog fled in horror, panic rising in his gorge like bile, just as he wished to flee now.

Bear Dog lifted his muzzle and, circling the pit floor, howled once again. Now the steel cage was settling slowly onto the bottom, one reinforced metal corner at a time. Suddenly Bear Dog halted his frantic circling and stopped his baying. He hunkered down in a corner of the enclosed arroyo, hackles lifting and rippling, teeth bared, muzzle foaming, eyes blazing.

Torturously and with crucifying lassitude, the slack, looped lass rope that was secured to the dead-fall door pulled taut.

Then the door opened.

And the griz was loose.

13

The two waited for a long, hellish moment. Bear Dog was flattened on the pit floor; Tiny was up on his hind legs. Each knew his fate. The griz would prevail; Bear Dog would die. Bear Dog knew it. The griz in his agony knew it.

But as they stared into the blazing eternity of each other's eyes, another truth was revealed.

Ursus horribilis would pay dearly for that death.

Bear Dog made the first move. In a spectacular twelve-foot leap across the pit, he hit the bayed Tiny squarely on the most sensitive part of his body, a portion of the anatomy even more sensitive than his testicles.

His nose.

His massive jaws clamped onto the muzzle, tight as a vise.

The response from the boar griz was instantaneous. He could not stand there with two hundred pounds of dog meat hanging from his tender nose. He dropped to all fours and launched himself like a howitzer straight at the arroyo wall.

And battered both himself and Bear Dog into unconsciousness.

The crowd, howling crazily around the top of the pit, hushed. From their vantage point it appeared that both animals had been killed. For a long minute they paused to reconsider their bets.

Bear Dog was the first to stir. This led to instant cheers from Lorenzo and hooting derision from the rest. And when Bear Dog rose, he did not shake his head and gaze around stupidly.

He went straight for the throat of the supine grizzly.

The dog's fangs slashed deeply into the dense neck fur, and Tiny's rich brown coat was instantly showered with crimson gore. Incredibly, the attack revived the griz. Now he rolled over onto his stomach, crushing the dog; then, getting his legs under him, he rose on his haunches.

It was a macabre death dance. The dog hanging there with his muzzle still locked on the bear's throat, hoping against hope for some break in the heavy carapace of skin, grinding inexorably toward Tiny's jugular.

Nor was the griz passive. He had the hanging dog locked in a hug that should have cracked an anvil.

But not Bear Dog.

The loss of blood from Tiny's gnawed throat and the twisting tourniquet of neck skin strangling his windpipe were taking their toll.

The dog and the griz hung there dancing and floundering across the pit floor, locked forever in their lethal embrace. On and on they stumbled, till the bear could take no more. Hindquarters buckling, lungs gasping, Tiny had to make a move. Lifting the dog horizontally in front of his body, the grizzly went to the arroyo wall. There, he repeatedly slammed the dog's back against the sandstone facing. Each blow twisted and ripped Tiny's neck wounds wider, but still the bear slammed.

At the fourth blow the dog's jaws released, and he slid into unconsciousness. The grizzly, bleeding profusely from the nose, ears, and throat, fell backward.

A dead-still hush came over the crowd above. They feared that both beasts had died simultaneously, and it did seem that way. The two lay there inert, the dog's muzzle less than a foot from the supine grizzly's spread hind legs. The two animals looked as if they'd been riddled by Gatlings. Their blood was everywhere. The pit floor, walls, and the coats of the two animals were dense with crimson gore.

After a seeming eternity, Bear Dog—to the savage yells of his topside supporters—raised his muzzle.

Bear Dog thought, Well, you've given him everything you have. You matched him strength for strength, fang for fang, pound for pound.

You can't overwhelm him.

He's too big and too tough.

Bear Dog simply lay there, watching his adversary, the massive trunk, the huge head, the stumpy legs.

Less than a foot from Tiny's outflung hindquarters, he studied the grizzly's tremendous genitals. The griz was flat on his back.

Plan became action.

He reared back on his haunches and sprang at the grizzly's groin.

With one savage slash the unconscious grizzly was castrated.

Testicles, penis, all.

Instantly the griz was on all fours, then up on

his haunches, pawing madly at his blood-gushing crotch.

Bear Dog went once more for the throat in a straight-forward lunge. Again he caught the wounded neck, now torn wide open, and got his purchase. He ripped his way a millimeter at a time toward the jugular in a shower of blood.

Now Bear Dog had him. He could sense it. Tiny was not trying to crush him in a death hug but instead pawed feebly at his crotch. Bear Dog knew that in just a few seconds more he would slash the jugular. He knew it. The griz knew he could.

Then it happened.

Tiny went down, just like that.

He went down. Like a hammered steer. Like a collapsing bridge. Muzzle first onto the pit floor.

Onto Bear Dog.

At first the dog thought this was another of Tiny's ploys, and he only intensified the pressure on Tiny's throat. Then he noticed that Tiny was no longer struggling.

Tiny was no longer moving.

Tiny lay there like a stone.

Tiny was dead.

Suddenly, Bear Dog hit it. At the precise moment when he realized the griz was dead, he bit through the jugular vein and carotid artery. Those massive vessels were filled with collosal quantities of blood, and when they ruptured, the twin conduits fountained straight

into Bear Dog's mouth and down his throat and
windpipe.

And there he lay, hopelessly pinned under a
half-ton grizzly bear, drowning in the dead beast's
blood.

14

When Flynn, Slater, Flaco, and the rest of the
band rode up the winding gorge onto the high,
virtually impregnable mountain cliff that was
the Comancheros' permanent camp, they were
surprised by the absence of sentries. When they
finished the last steep leg of the narrow trail,
hand leading their mounts, and still found no
guards, Flynn was alarmed. They checked their
weapons, jacked rounds into the chambers of
their Winchesters, and slipped through the narrow defile onto the clifftop.

At the far end of the camp was the rest of the
Comanchero band, mobbed around the gaming
pit, laughing, drinking, gambling.

Flynn swung back onto his gray, his face working in rage. Slater vaulted the roan and pulled
up alongside him.

"What's up?" asked Slater.

"I don't know, but this 'no sentry' shit don't cut it."

"That haired-over hardcase of yours, Lorenzo, he the one s'posed to be in charge? The one with the man-killin' dog?"

"You got it."

"You sure he ain't no friend of yours?"

"I told you once I don't have any friends."

They pulled up alongside the crowd, swung off, and shouldered their way in, Flaco behind them. When they got to the rim of the twenty-foot pit, Flynn strode up to a man in greasy buckskins with an Arbuckle's bag full of double eagles, pesos, and greenbacks in one hand and a jug of tequila in the other. The man was obviously drunk.

"Lorenzo," Flynn asked calmly, "where are the sentries? Nobody's watching the pass."

Lorenzo smiled feebly, drunkenly. "They was makin' book."

Flynn looked perplexed. "On what?"

"On that." Lorenzo pointed down into the pit. "I pitted that damn Bear Dog against a griz. He whipped him, too, 'ceptin' the damn thing fell on him. Crushed the life out of him."

Flynn looked even more perplexed. "You mean you took your own animal, the personal protector of your property, a hound who was the camp's guard dog, best tracker and hunter, and you let a grizzly kill him for sport?"

"Fuck him. He was just a dog. And now he's a dead dog."

"You sure he's dead?" Slater asked.

"Ton of grizzly on him? Hell yes, he's dead."

"You go down there and look?"

"Hell no. I know that dog's through. Just ain't sure yet about the griz."

Slater stared at Lorenzo in disbelief. He said to Flynn, "You sure he ain't no friend of yours?"

Flynn glared at Slater. "How many times I got to tell you?"

Slater looked back at Lorenzo. "I think you better go down there and check."

"S'posin' I don't want to?"

Slater shrugged his shoulders slowly, as if working a kink out of his back muscles. "Okay by me." Then he hammered Lorenzo as hard as he knew how with a looping left hook, driving him over the edge of the pit. Tumbling head over heels, the only thing that broke his fall on the hard bottom was the spread body of the dead griz.

Slater turned and pulled a Winchester out of his saddle sheath. Slinging it over his shoulder, he grabbed on to one of the cage ropes, which was still harnessed to the mules. He swung out over the pit and slid down the rope.

Down in the pit, he placed the muzzle of the Winchester against the back of the bear's head and pumped in three rounds, figuring that would hold him. He considered doing the same to the out-cold Lorenzo, but instead rolled his body off the bear.

He pulled an Arkansas toothpick out of his back sheath and severed the cage rope. He beckoned the line down farther, and Flaco, up top, complied. When he had enough slack, he lashed the line around the grizzly's bloody head and under his armpits. After tying the line off, he motioned it back up.

The mules hit their chest harnesses and collars. Slowly the grizzly moved. When Tiny was half-up, Slater pulled Bear Dog out from under the grizzly.

Slater got down and listened to the dog's chest. God only knew how much internal damage had been done and how many bones had been broken. Still, the dog's heart was beating, and the eyelids fluttered once.

The chief problem, Slater saw quickly, was that the dog's throat and trachea were filled with blood. Slater considered the problem, then remembered that when newborn pups choked on afterbirth, the bitches would shake them till the afterbirth tumbled out. He ordered the rope back down, cut it off the now-prone bear, and secured it to the dog's hindquarters.

After he had Bear Dog hoisted upside down, the blood began trickling out his nose and mouth. Slater did not know whether it was the grizzly's or Bear Dog's but this was no time for fine distinctions. He slapped the dog on the chest and back.

Slowly, huge gouts of gore began streaming out of his throat and windpipe.

Grizzly gore.

When the last of the blood was out, the dog breathed steadily, if weakly. Slater yelled up, "Hey, amigo, drop down a couple of planks."

In a few minutes two good-size boards tumbled into the pit. Slater eased the dog onto the planks and secured them with both the cage and the dead-fall ropes.

He motioned the makeshift scaffold on up. As it started to move, he climbed on, his legs straddling the still-breathing animal. Once, as they neared the top, the dog lifted his head, fixed Slater with a long, slow stare, then laid his head sideways on the planks. The dog's eyes seemed to Slater sleepy, dreamy, yet penetrating, as if the dog was trying to comprehend what was happening.

When they reached topside, Slater, with help from Flaco, carried Bear Dog on his makeshift stretcher away from the pit.

PART VI

15

On a small hill outside Brownsville, Texas, two dozen troopers broke camp and cinched up their mounts. The horses were common unbranded bays. The troopers were all dressed the same: sky-blue trousers, hickory shirts with wide suspenders, tight blouses of dark blue flannel, and black knee-high boots. Their kossuth hats were pinned up rakishly along the right side with the insignia of two crossed rifles. Army Colts were strapped to their hips, butts turned out, but instead of the usual Springfield .56s slung muzzle-down across their backs, they had saddle-sheathed repeating Winchesters. The saddles were McClellans.

Three men stood apart from all this frenzied activity. All were officers. The bearded one wore eagles on his shoulders, the rank of a bird colonel. The decidedly Latin-looking officer wore double captain's bars, while the big man with broad shoulders and astonishingly flat, black eyes wore the oak-leaf clusters of a major.

However, if one looked closely at these uniforms, there were definite peculiarities. Each of the cavalry blouses had one or more charred, sometimes reddish holes in the front and larger apertures in the back. Some of the rips had been scrubbed around the edges with cold water in an attempt to remove the strange crimson stains. A few of the holes had actually been patched. But the repair jobs had been sloppy, the sort of slipshod work one might expect from men who had no real feel for darning and sewing, for hearth and home.

In fact, these were not troopers at all.

The three standing around the fire were Jim Flynn, Bloody Flaco and the outlaw Torn Slater.

The rest were Comancheros.

16

"Goddamn," Flynn grumbled to the two men squatting with him around the dying campfire. "We ambush and kill two dozen troopers, steal a fucking Gatling off an arms train." He nodded to the hundred-caliber gun turreted on its double wheels. "Now we prepare to rob a bank, protected by half a garrison of blue-bellies?"

"And we paid his amigo, the gunrunner Carpenter, *muchos* pesos for this brilliant plan," Flaco added.

Torn Slater shrugged. "You wanted in that bank. You wanted that one-fifty thou. You got to go in and take it. Ain't no other way. So how else you gonna do it? Only people getting close to that bank with any freedom at all is the fuckin' army."

"You don't leave a man much of a choice, do you?" said Flynn.

"Shotgun choice," Flaco said. "And if you ask me, it don't matter much which barrel you pick. They both look eight-gauge."

"No percentage in leavin' men a choice," said Slater.

Flynn fixed Slater with an appraising stare. "You really don't give a damn, do you? You've lost so much that can never be replaced, it just don't make any difference. Whether you live, die, or do time, it's all the same."

Slater rose and headed toward his mount.

The two others followed Slater to the horses. All three swung on and trotted to the head of the line.

Flaco turned and looked at the troop nervously. "I still say we could use some more help we gonna take that bank."

Flynn shook his head. "We don't need help. We need a Bible."

17

Two dozen hard-looking troopers rode up the center of Main Street, pulling a double-wheeled hundred-caliber Gatling gun. Their colonel was a somber gent in a full beard, a man with a no-nonsense look about him. As officers from the nearby garrison rode past and saluted, they may have had reservations about the slovenly demeanor of his troop. Among other things, the colonel's men rode with their hats pulled down rakishly over their eyes in direct contravention of army regulations. But as to the seriousness of the colonel there could be no doubt. This was a can-do sort of soldier, a man in Brownsville on business.

So they rode into town unimpeded. When they reached the front of the Brownsville Guarantee and Trust and the colonel raised his right hand and barked the command to halt, no one paid notice.

When the colonel, major, and captain marched with confident, military authority into the bank, the passersby did not even give them a second glance.

If anything, they felt relief.

The United States Army was bringing law and order to Brownsville, Texas.

18

Inside, tellers in three cages, wearing white boiled shirts, celluloid collars, and black elbow garters, worked feverishly. Behind them was a spacious office for the bank president. In the bull pen, a clerk with a green eyeshade was working on the books. An unlit coal-oil lamp hung from the ceiling. A cuspidor stood by the door. On the wall was a sepia portrait of Jefferson Davis.

The colonel made his intentions clear to the head teller, who stood soberly in his cage.

"Sir, we have important business to discuss with the president of this bank. It involves the security of your depositors and the safety of everyone employed here."

"You mean there could be another holdup now that Torn Slater's broke out of jail?"

"What I mean, my good man, is that we need a full quarter hour alone with your president. Alone and undisturbed."

The teller pointed to the president's office, directly in back of his cage. "He's in there with the door closed, but he's busy."

"Oh, he won't be too busy to see us," said the rough-looking major with the low-brimmed hat, short-cropped beard, and flat, black eyes. "Not when he recognizes how important the situation is."

"Indeed," the colonel concurred. "And please, a good quarter of an hour. Undisturbed. We are expecting trouble, and we must all move fast." The colonel turned to the captain. "Perhaps you could help the teller here to see that we are not interrupted."

The captain grinned and saluted. "Yes, sir."

Later, it would seem to the head teller that the captain's grin had held more than a hint of wickedness.

19

They went in single file, Gentleman Jim Flynn, the colonel, leading the way. Torn Slater kept well to the rear.

Both wore their hats pulled low.

The bank president was a balding man in a black frock coat, a matching black vest, and a white boiled shirt. He wore Benjamin Franklin spectacles and a celluloid collar. He was dictating a letter to an assistant in a white linen shirt, elbow garters, and a bow tie. The assistant turned his head as they entered. The bank president was confused. He clearly was not used to interruptions.

"Officers, can I help you?"

"You sure fucking can," snapped the major to the rear, his voice like a whip crack.

H. Howard Jones was startled by the major's tone and instantly he knew something was wrong. Very wrong. Not only were these men breaching every rule of banking decorum—by crashing into his office—but there was something else. Very simply, he did not like the way they looked.

He stood abruptly and started to call for the head teller. He would demand an explanation this very second.

But H. Howard Jones was too slow.

The big major directly behind the colonel was already across the room and around the desk, moving faster than he'd ever seen a big man move before. Furthermore, the colonel now had the assistant—who was already trembling and whimpering—by the nape. In the same motion he kicked the door shut behind him, then chair-locked it.

"Hi, Howard," the big man said. "Long time no see."

Howard stared into the flat black eyes of the major—no more major than he was. He winced at the arrogant grin, his mistake now glaringly apparent.

Outlaw Torn Slater!

"You filthy, miserable, murdering—"

He got no further. A nonregulation navy Colt

came whipping out from the belt beneath the major's blouse. The barrel struck him twice—backhand and forehand.

The razor-sharp sight sliced the cheeks with each blow, laying them wide open. Howard started to cry out, but then the muzzle shattered three teeth and rammed the back of his mouth, effectively muffling all protests. Slater then savagely worked the filed sight around the interior of Howard's mouth, ripping into the roof, slashing through the lip, and tearing open the inside of the cheek. Slater shoved the barrel as far down Howard's throat as it would go, till he was gagging bile and blood, and his face was streaked with gore. Slater's hand was under Howard's chin, jerking his head back over the top of his plush desk chair. He slammed it into the back of the wall. Slater was talking softly, very softly, over his shoulder to the colonel.

"Remember I told you about the one-way back-stabbing son of a bitch who set me up for that last bank job? The one who talked *me* into robbin' the place, then put the gold double eagles on top and left me with fucking washers underneath? And who then ratted me out to the law? I'd like you to meet the man, Mr. H. Howard Jones. And that blubbering wreck you hold trembling in your own hands? His accomplice, Paul Tarpin."

Howard wanted to say something, but the navy Colt was ramming the back of his throat.

Paul continued to blubber.

"Okay, honcho," Slater said coolly, "where's the fuckin' pesos?"

Slowly the bank president shook his head.

No.

Everybody had to admit the guy had stones. To sit there with a cocked navy Colt in your mouth, a murdering outlaw on the other end, and still lie about knowing the whereabouts of other people's money took a certain kind of guts.

Unfortunately for Howard and for the Brownsville Guarantee and Trust, it was not the kind of guts Torn Slater respected. He glanced over his shoulder at Flynn, who had a bandanna stuffed into Tarpin's mouth and the man's hands tied behind his back.

Slater said tonelessly, "Kill the assistant. Cut his fuckin' throat. Maybe that'll jar this asshole's memory."

Paul Tarpin was not quite as concerned about the bank's finances as his boss was. He began shaking his head wildly, pointing at a Navajo rug beneath their feet.

Flynn looked at Slater.

Slater shrugged. "Pick it up and see."

Shoving the assistant's face to the wall, right alongside a steel engraving of Ulysses Simpson Grant, Flynn grabbed the rug and flung it aside.

Underneath was a trapdoor.

"Nice, very nice," Slater said, genuinely impressed. "A second vault, huh? One you never described to your old buddy Slater. Well, I guess you're about to tell him now, huh, Howard?"

The assistant, still gagged, face to the wall, was nodding his frantic agreement.

Flynn already had the trap up. He was staring into the dark depths where a ladder descended. Hanging alongside the ladder was a coal-oil hand lamp, which Flynn promptly lit. Then, grabbing Tarpin by the back of the shirt, he shoved him down the ladder. He quickly followed, the president and Slater in tow, Slater closing the trap after him.

20

With the trap and office doors shut, the four of them were soundproofed from the bank lobby. And since Tarpin seemed the more talkative, Flynn pulled out the gag.

In the glaring light of the coal-oil lamp, he examined the basement. It wasn't much. Adobe walls and some sort of brick floor. Two varnished-pine file cabinets, a rolltop desk that looked to be good oak, and a few crates of paper. Another Navajo rug was spread out under their feet.

Flynn returned his attention to the assistant. Somehow he seemed to have acquired a little more backbone. His eyes no longer darted as nervously. The tremor in his hands subsided.

Flynn assumed that Slater would change all that.

Which he did.

This time Slater drove the muzzle of his navy Colt into the assistant's mouth. Flynn was satisfied when Tarpin began to cry.

Slowly, carefully, Flynn pulled Slater off the sobbing assistant.

Slater returned to the president and put the muzzle of the gun in his nose.

"Now, Paul," Flynn said softly to the young man, the slightest hint of a brogue in his voice, "I'm sure you're a good boy and would like to do the right thing." Paul nodded, his eyes swimming with tears. "But you see, my friend there, he's very impulsive, you know? Many bad things have happened to him in regard to this bank. Men have died and done time because of the money here and your employer across the room. And if you two do not come up with the cash that my friend and I believe is rightfully ours, that man across this small dark basement will do some very bad things. Take my word, this is no idle threat. He will make you curse your mother for giving you birth."

"The rug," Paul sniveled. "There's a floor safe under the rug. That's where we keep the really big accounts."

"Now there's a fine boy," Flynn said, gently patting Paul on the cheek. "A good act of contrition." Slater bent down and jerked up the rug.

The floor safe had a square door, two feet on an edge.

And a combination lock.

"Now, Paul, my boy," Flynn continued gently, "we must have the combination. Oh, I do suppose we could blast or peel our way into the damn thing, but we have neither the time, facilities, nor the inclination. So if you please, the combination. And we are in a bit of a hurry."

"Howard," Paul said imploringly, "give it to them. You know I don't know it."

"You slimy coward," Howard said.

"Please, give it to them. My wife, my children, my mother . . . I don't want to die." He dropped to the floor. He was trying to clutch Flynn's knees in supplication. Flynn glanced down at him in disgust and kicked him in the neck.

"Howard, you sure this dude doesn't know the combination?" Slater asked.

Howard looked offended. "Do you think I would be dumb enough to give anything that valuable to *that*?"

"I suppose not," Slater agreed.

"In which case a small object lesson?" Flynn suggested pleasantly.

Slater nodded.

Flynn regarded the unconscious Paul, then stripped the frock coat off Howard. He wrapped it around the muzzle of his own Colt .45 to stifle the noise. Placing the barrel over the kneecap of the unconscious assistant, he shot him in the knee.

It was as if Paul had turned into a bomb and exploded. He thrashed around the floor, which was rapidly being covered with his blood. Flynn frantically beat Howard's flaming coat against the walls to put out the fire.

Finally, Flynn silenced Tarpin by clamping a boot heel over his throat. When he turned to Slater, Howard was bent backward over the desk. Flynn took over. He shoved the muzzle of the Colt into Howard's crotch. In a voice that was deceptively soothing, Flynn talked to him.

"As I recall, the last man I had bent over this desk here was Paul, and if you don't tell me that combination, to say that isn't going to be you wallowing around on the floor, well, that would be just plain unrealistic. So which is it going to be? The combination or your balls?"

It never occurred to Flynn that when Howard spat in his face, he was showing real *cojones*. At the time, it just seemed stupid. Flynn's only response was to snake the long narrow blade of the Arkansas toothpick out of his forearm sheath and drive it through Howard's elbow straight into the rolltop desk.

He left it there, thrumming violently.

Flynn jammed his forearm against Howard's windpipe so that the man was not only in blinding, speechless agony, he was suffocating.

"You hear me, Howard?"

Incredibly enough, Howard again spat in Flynn's face.

Flynn removed his arm from the man's windpipe and jiggled the blade, jacking up the level of pain. Vomit oozed out of Howard's mouth and nose, and his bladder emptied.

Flynn looked at his watch. It was going too slowly. They'd been in the basement twelve minutes and still no gold. Again he wrapped the charred coat around his .45. He went up to Howard.

"See this?" Flynn said, thrusting the wrapped-up pistol under Howard's nose.

Howard sobbed his understanding, then once more spat in Flynn's face.

Flynn shot out Howard's left kneecap.

Howard immediately convulsed in agony, and Slater grabbed him. It took every ounce of Slater's strength to hold him up against the rolltop desk while Flynn again beat out the flames of the badly charred frock coat. Then he rewrapped the gun barrel and once more thrust it under Howard's nose.

"Ready again?" Flynn asked.

Howards lips moved. They were bloodlessly white and streaked with puke. His eyes had the crazed look of a caged ape, but the lips were trying to say something. The word looked like *please.* Flynn moved Slater aside and took Slater's pistol out of Howard's mouth.

"Please...Bible," were Howard's only words.

Slater started to work the knife again when Flynn saw a leather-bound copy of the King James Bible on one of the filing cabinets.

"Wait," he said, staying Slater's hand.

Flynn got the Bible and shoved it under Howard's face.

Howard nodded.

Flynn heard indistinctly: "Matthew...twenty-two...twenty-one..."

Frantically Flynn began riffling the pages. Bingo. There, precisely at Matthew 22:21, he found the verse: "Render therefore unto Caesar what is Caesar's."

And in the margin?

2 left, 4 right, 7 left.

Instantly Flynn was down on his hands and knees.

Almost as fast, the lock clicked and the safe opened.

Suddenly he heard a thud and spun around, his gun cocked. H. Howard Jones had just fallen to the floor, his throat cut.

Flynn nodded and did likewise to Paul.

So much for the informant.

And the accomplice.

He returned to the safe. It looked promising, but still he could not forget Slater's bags full of washers. This safe too was filled with big canvas bags, knotted at the top. Quickly he untied the drawstrings and sifted through the contents.

Double eagles, greenbacks, and bearer bonds.

Clean clear through.

Hundreds of thousands of dollars' worth.

21

It took less than eight and a half minutes for six Comancheros to empty the floor safe. Gentleman Jim Flynn stayed in the bank lobby, explaining the operation to the head teller.

"You see, young man, the situation here is grave. We have explained the facts in detail to the good Mr. Jones and his associate, Mr. Tarpin. Unfortunately, this dastardly band of Comancheros, headed up by none other than the infamous outlaw Torn Slater, have set their sights on this bank. Revenge on the part of Slater, no doubt. Uncontrollable greed on the part of those other nefarious outlaws. We all felt the bank's holdings would be safer at the fort. Mr. Jones agreed. He and Mr. Tarpin, even as we speak, are supervising the transferal of those funds from a clandestine vault in the cellar. Very clever, that extra vault."

Flynn took out a pocket watch and glanced at the time. It was a B. W. Raymond key winder with a hinged lid and an eight-day movement. The winding key hung from the chain.

It was a railroad timepiece, forcibly donated to Flynn by a conductor on the Union Pacific.

"Not much longer, then we'll be leaving. Uh, by the way, my good man, if you have other excess capital, which you fear for, you may also pack it up. We can put it in 'protective custody,' so to speak."

In less than twenty minutes they were gone.

22

The military-looking troop of tricked-out Comancheros, riding two abreast, had almost reached the end of the dusty Main Street.

When they ran into a band of fifty Texas Rangers.

This largely voluntary organization had fought outlaws and renegades long before the U.S. Army had even dreamed of coming to Texas. Moreover, they were, in the main, unforgiving Confederates and lost no love on troopers.

The ranger captain was a notorious blue-belly–hating ex-rebel named Nelson Longtree. He'd fought under General Jo Shelby and had even gone to Mexico with him after the war to continue the struggle.

He'd also fought beside Slater.

And knew him well.

Seeing Longtree approach from up the street, Slater dropped back to the middle of the troop.

Closer to the Gatling gun.

The rangers were in civilian garb but each had a Lone Star badge gleaming on his chest, pinned above the heart.

Flynn saluted Longtree on the way out of town and attempted to continue on his way, but Longtree waved him down. Flynn halted the troop. "I'd be most pleased to stop for a chat, Captain. Unfortunately, duty calls, and we are on important business."

"Yeah? Well hold your water, hoss, jus' one minute. I got important business too. You men heard anything 'bout that massacre of two dozen blue-bellies up Neuces way less'n a week ago?"

"Yes, a very unfortunate situation. Now, my good man, if you'll only yield the street, we'll be on—"

"Yeah," Longtree interrupted in a dead-flat panhandle drawl, "two dozen blue-bellies found shot to death, half-buried, stripped of their uniforms, supplies, and also a hundred-caliber Gatling gun. Which is a mighty high caliber for a Gatling. Say, that ain't a Gatling you got right there, is it? Couldn't be a hundred caliber neither?"

"My good man, as of this moment you are interfering with army officers in the performance of their duty, and if you do not clear the way instantly, I shall—"

"Say, Colonel, that's a might interestin' tear you got in the middle of your blouse. Kind of reddish-looking and charred around the edges. You wouldn't mind me looking at the back, would you?"

"If you must know, I was severely wounded at the Battle of Adobe Walls, some years ago. Now, if you would only—"

"Say," Longtree interrupted again, "who's that haired-over hardcase down there by the Gatling? What's a fucking major doing so far back in the line? Say, Harve," Longtree shouted back to his lieutenant, "you fought under Quantrill and Bloody Bill. I personally only met the man eight or ten times, but don't that major by the Gatling bear an ugly resemblance to ol' Torn Slater?"

Suddenly, all fifty rangers were going for their guns, and at the same instant Slater was diving off his mount, straight for the Gatling. He reached the crank just as the first rangers cleared their guns. Instantly he had the handle turning, going directly for the greatest concentration of rangers, the ones clogging the center of the street.

If they had refused to give way before, they yielded the road now.

Not that they had much choice. The Gatling's high-powered rounds—four times larger than those of a "Big Fifty" Sharps—tore through the densely packed ranger company like miniature cannonballs. Those who caught more than one round were virtually dismembered. The psychological effect of that 1,500-round-per-minute buzzsaw ripping through their ranks was shattering.

Before Slater was halfway through the drum, fragments of ranger bodies and limbs—whole hands, feet, even heads—were flying through the air. Dense whitish clouds of black-powder smoke hung over the main stem, scorching the throat, stinging and blinding the eyes. Ears rang and pounded, and the rangers no longer attempted to return the fire.

They raced for cover, any cover. Water troughs, barrels, hitchracks, corners of buildings, anything, anywhere to escape the savage hammering of the Gatling.

Not that it did much good. Whatever cover they found disintegrated to sawdust under the Gatling's pounding. As for the Comancheros, they were hardly idle during the slaughter. With Slater backing them up and the rangers in full rout, Flynn, Flaco, and the rest picked off the escaping rangers like clay pigeons.

It was less a rout than a massacre.

The few who died fell only because they could not clear the street in time and were hit by the Gatling.

It was over in less than fifteen seconds. More than sixty bodies and at least as many horses lay strewn across the Brownsville street. The few who made it to some sort of shelter lay dead behind their shattered barricades.

Among them lay Longtree, who, after taking two in the neck, was missing his head. Flynn, coldly, without thinking, reloaded his horse pistols. Glancing over his shoulder, he observed Slater shove another drum into the Gatling's smoking breech. Slater then remounted his horse, which Flaco had brought to him. When they rejoined Flynn at the head of the troop, the buzzards were already starting to circle.

Flaco glanced up. "This is mighty sudden country."

Flynn nodded. "Only for the quick. For the dead it seems kind of slow."

"I be your witness there," said Slater.

Flynn raised his right arm cavalry-fashion and shouted to his troop, "Line 'em up and head 'em on out."

"Damn, amigo, you really get into this cavalry shit," Flaco said to Flynn.

Flynn looked back at Slater and Flaco. "Ah yes. *Veni, vidi, vici.*' 'I came, I saw, I conquered.' The profession of arms. It does get to you after a while. I see us as one of the empire's proud legions, don't you agree?"

"I just see us countin' them pesos," Slater said.

The Comancheros rode on out of town.

Slowly, the swirling funnel-shaped cloud of vultures descended over Brownsville.

PART VII

23

They'd been six days on the owlhoot and were deep into Mexico before Flynn and Slater thought it prudent to rest. They camped in a narrow canyon in the Chihuahua desert, picketed and rubbed down their mounts, then grained and watered them. Flaco built a small smokeless fire, brewed their first coffee, and cooked their first hot food in close to a week.

At dawn, Flynn approached Slater. He was near the remuda, getting set to cinch up.

"Sport, there's something I want to show you down the pass. Flaco spotted it last night."

Flaco stood beside Flynn and nodded gravely.

"Come on, friend. Just the three of us. I don't want the rest of these fools wising up."

Slater nodded and followed them.

The narrow pass zigged and zagged and then took a sharp right turn. Flynn pointed to a pile of boulders and said, "Look at that."

When Slater turned toward the boulders, his head exploded. Then a second time, then a third.

He plunged into swirling, agonizing blackness.

After a long time the pain whirled and brightened into a vast circle of light. After an eternity of waiting, the light began to shrink. Soon it was little more than the small circle in a bull's-eye lantern. Then it diminished till it was the size of a pinhead, then a pinprick, then just an infinitesimal dot.

Suddenly, the light went out.

And Slater knew no more.

24

When he came to, Slater was buck-naked, flat on his back, and Flaco was staking him out. He still had one more foot to go. He was hammering an X-shaped pair of foot-and-a-half pegs over his left ankle. Like his other limbs, it was about to be lashed to the crossed stakes. Flynn was straddling his legs, a stagged-off eight-gauge Greener in his right fist. The muzzle dangled over his balls.

"I wouldn't try anything, sport. Certainly not until Flaco has finished. First of all, you can't get away with it. Secondly, I have just enough cayenne and lye in these barrels to make you very sorry you tried."

Slater was silent.

When Flaco finished, Flynn said with just a hint of the brogue, "Now, there's a good lad. I'm so pleased we could do this with a minimum of fuss. You know how I abhor a spot of bother."

Slater attempted to ask *Why?* But his head was swimming, his vision blurred. He couldn't get the word out.

Flynn nodded knowingly. "I'm afraid our colleague Flaco hit you a little too forcefully. He had you by the hip, so to speak, and was afraid if he didn't put you down hard, you might rise to fight another day. Understandable as his motives were, I wish he hadn't done that. I wanted you staked out like a spread-eagled barn owl, limbs splendidly outflung, but still at the height of your powers, able to savor every moment of this exquisite delight. I'm afraid, however, that you might have a bit of trouble with that gash. It extends from your chin, well past your ear, into your temple. From the looks of all that blood welling in it, there could be some pain." Flynn paused, bent over Slater, and peered closely into the deep, dark cut. "Ah, there's a good boy. It's clotting now. Rather nicely, too. I'm afraid you've concussed, old friend, but no help for that now."

This time Slater got it out: "Why?"

"Yes, that must puzzle you. After all, you required none of the loot. Certainly none of the first hundred and fifty thou. But even if the motive were money, why go to these lengths? Wouldn't it be easier just to back shoot you on the trail?"

Slater thought, Yes, it would have been easier.

"So, in truth, I do have other motivation. You, Flaco, and I were not the only men who wanted the money out of that bank. There was another— the one who collected all that insurance the first time around and then had the *cojones* to defraud *Mejico's presidente,* Porfirio Diaz. It seems Diaz as well as Lloyd's of London was more than a little suspicious of that last job of work. They both wanted a closer look at the bank's records. Quite frankly, the bank's real owner wanted the funds transferred someplace safer and more discreet. Say to a bank in Switzerland. Unfortunately, all those double eagles are extremely heavy, hard to move, and really need a great deal of protection. This was not the sort of transfer that the owner could effect, say, under cover of dark with a carpetbag. Furthermore, there was the matter of that insurance policy he'd taken out with Lloyd's of London after the other job. It was so tempting to hit the bank again, and sting those damnable limeys twice, don't you agree?"

"Why me?" Slater croaked.

"Simple. You're the best bank man in the country. If anyone could figure a way to rob that place, you could. And indeed our friend was right."

"Why *this*?" Slater croaked.

Flynn grinned broadly. "Well, it seems the clandestine owner of that Brownsville bank has a little grudge against you, you know? Seems you and he had a small disagreement a few years back. You half-scalped him and hung him by the hocks over a slow-burning fire. He's never forgiven you for that little practical joke. Still quite angry about it. Wants to repay the compliment. So this is part of my rather considerable fee. A few days from now I shall meet Mr. Sutherland, then bring him back here. He says he will piss on your sun-scorched, ant-gnawed remains and gloat. But don't take it too hard, sport. By then you won't care, will you?"

Now Slater's voice and vision were clearing. "I didn't think you had it in you, Flynn. Not *this*."

"Don't blame me, my friend. It was you who chose to bargain your soul against worldly riches."

"But not *this*. An Apache would do it, yes. But no white man."

"Old friend, never believe you know the last word of any human heart."

Slater could already feel the sun burning into his retinas and his limbs growing cramped. In an hour's time God only knew what he would feel.

Especially if the ants got to him.

God no, not the ants.

For one terrible moment of panic, Slater wanted only to die.

"Say, old son, I hope you aren't about to ask for mercy, are you?" Flynn asked.

Now that his vision had cleared, Slater saw that all the Comancheros were gathered around. They laughed hackingly at Flynn's gibes. Lorenzo, whom he'd knocked into the gaming pit, strode up and booted him in the ribs.

Flaco hammered Lorenzo in the side of the neck with everything he had, knocking him ass over teakettle across the arroyo.

"Good man, Flaco," Flynn said, glancing disdainfully at the unconscious Lorenzo lying against the arroyo wall. "I, too, deplore poor sportsmanship."

"You better kill me, Flynn. I'll get you for this," said Slater.

"Well done, ducks. I adore bravado in the face of death. But you shan't get anyone. And please don't injure yourself straining against these stakes. My colleagues are most adept in these matters." Flynn stretched, lifted his head, and smiled brightly. Still grinning, he glanced down at Slater. "You know, I am pleased that you don't expect mercy from these people or from me. I would have been most embarrassed if Outlaw Torn Slater's last words had been filled with begging and whimpering. Quite frankly, I shall be delighted to report to this Sutherland chap that at the very end you were stout as a lion."

"Really white of you, Flynn."

"I know. The weight of failure is hard to bear. When you are gone, just another rejected remnant of the male gender, nobody will care, will they? What will accompany Torn Slater on this crossing of the bar? Muted minor chords? Eternal ecstasy? Or just a shrill scream, a gathering silence, and the rest, nothing?"

"Flynn, it don't end here."

"But it does, my friend. You are on the Death Ship of the Ancient Mariner. You are destined for wherever it is the dead go. That is all. Oh yes, there's a lot more I could tell you about these matters, but there's no need now. Take my word. Soon you shall have a more authoritative answer."

"Flynn, fuck off."

"Yes, it is time for that," said Flynn, opening the hinged-lid of his B. W. Raymond railroad watch. "I do wish we had had more of a chance to chat. Perhaps send you off with a truly dramatic flourish. You know? 'Could not all this flesh keep in a little life? Poor Torn, farewell, I could have better spared a better man.'"

Slater tried to turn his head away from the grinning Irishman, but was restrained by the crossed stakes. Flynn bent over him till they were nearly nose to nose. He patted his cheek gently.

"Say, I really hope you're not bitter about any of this. Seriously. I'm as sorry to be going as you are to be staying. I'd love to stick around and witness your gradual deterioration, watch as you grow more anxious, more frightened, more critical of your former colleagues, more angry, more isolated, more dead. Regrettably, I have what you might call this sadistic streak. Flaco says it's a mile high and twice as wide. He says it has to do with a love of pain. In fact, it's a downright sexual love of it. Especially yours. So I really am sorry to be leaving you like this. I'd love to stay. There just isn't any more time."

"There'll be more time, Flynn. I promise you."

"Keep telling yourself that. Anything that keeps you going. Anything that prolongs the exquisiteness of this little *projet d'amour.* Pretend what you wish. And who knows? Perhaps you'll make it. Perhaps we shall meet again." Flynn shielded his eyes with his hands and stared east into the rising sun. He glanced back down at the spread-eagled Slater. "But, then again, perhaps we won't."

He waved the men toward the remuda while he continued to straddle Slater and grin. When the men all rounded the sharp bend, the grin fell away. He turned and walked back into the men's dust toward the breaking camp.

Without looking back.

PART VIII

25

Noontime in the arroyo.

The sun was at zenith, and Slater lay there stone-faced, the breeze whistling eerily through the slickrock canyons. He had lain there so quietly for so long that he was now just part of the landscape with no more identity than a rock.

For some time a kangaroo rat had been watching him as if trying to place this strange thing stretched out between crisscrossed wooden pegs.

Finally the rat lost interest and disappeared up the canyon.

All in all, Slater tried not to look at things like rats or boulders or canyon walls. Or the three shrunken, dehydrated flies diving and zooming around his blood-crusted head, their endless drone echoing in his ears like the mad buzzing whine of bumblebees. For the most part, he kept his eyes clenched shut. To open his eyes also entailed letting in the sun, Slater's bitterest enemy. To let it in meant exposing his retinas and optic nerves to its searing, blinding rays.

It was bad enough that the sun scorched and blistered his naked body. Here he lay, chest on fire, every nerve from the top of his skull to the base of his brain to the bottom of his spine to the soles of his feet utterly aflame. It was more than bad enough. But, had he exposed his eyeballs to the sun's naked rays, it would have led straight to madness.

Which he was rapidly approaching anyway.

That was what pained him most. Losing control of his mind, losing his awareness of events around him, and worse, not even caring. Those possibilities tortured him more than the sun. For in truth, he had always wanted in those final seconds to face the man or creature or thing that carved his scallop, to stare his nemesis dead in the eye and be utterly alert right up to the moment the lights went out. That had been more than his hope, it had been his profoundest wish, his most fervent prayer. Robbed of that faith, Slater did not know whether he could hold on to sanity or life.

He lay back, his eyes tightly closed, and tried to shut out the canyon that was now his entire world—his life, death, and tomb.

Growing weaker and weaker with each scorching minute, he willed himself not to give in to hallucination.

26

Dusk in the pit.

The westering sun was vibrant and vital. It hung suspended over the canyon's rim, a blazing kaleidoscope of red orange, yellow amber, and bloody gold. Then the rim raged with a flashfire of white-hot brimstone, sank behind the canyon wall, and was gone.

In the canyon all was dark and still. In the deepening twilight gloom, the walls cast wide black shadows over Slater, and slowly his sanity returned.

For a long time his mind had been reeling crazily, his thoughts fragmented and unfocused.

Now he could think again.

At first the sense of regaining control came to him as a relief. The ability to know who he was, what he was, where he was—things he'd been oblivious to these last several hours, the bearings and landmarks he needed.

Until he felt the pain.

His face, throat, chest, stomach, abdomen, genitals, legs, and feet were on fire. They were covered with what amounted to one raw, red, festering blister. His skin had gone beyond swarthy or red or even burned. He could describe it only as sun blackened. His face, from what he could feel of it, was gaunt, hollow cheeked, empty eyed, the nose and lips split and scorched.

And his tongue. Christ, his mouth had been dry before but never like this. His livid tongue lolled heavily in his mouth, raw, suppurating, as blistered as the sores on his body. The relentless. lash of the sun had cut him to the bone as deeply and painfully as any blacksnake whip.

His bloodshot eyes glared through their hooded lids at his lacerated body.

He might have been tempted by tears, but his eyes were too dehydrated.

He was tempted by every other kind of weakness—by anger, self-pity, and pride. Mostly by pride. He had always thought before that he could handle anything, anyone. He couldn't. He knew that now.

For the first time in his life, he felt old.

27

Darkness in the pit.

Not a darkness of the night so much as of the soul. The darkness of a man who has been broken on the rack and who knows in his heart that there is nothing left to fear or to hate or to love. Not a darkness of the night, which in the desert is awash in moonglow and the long blazing swath of the Milky Way, light brilliant enough to read by. No, a darkness of the heart.

Slowly, out of the depths of Slater's agony, he began to think. You, he thought bitterly, have had more than a nodding acquaintance with death. In Yuma and in the Sonoran Pit, you did your time. But you also knew hope. Yet here in this starlit night, you despair. Suppose, he thought, Flynn was right, that this experience is not something that one day you will recall and laugh at but one that will be etched in your soul, chiseled forever on the very halls of hell?

In this, his darkest moment, Slater tried to make himself aware of every aspect of his being and of the infernal pit. He became aware of his breath, now infinitesimally shallow, no longer calm breathing but muted, rattling gasps.

So be it.

He listened to the world around him. At first all he heard and felt were the muffled roaring in his ears, which was the pounding of his blood, and the hot needles of pain piercing his flesh.

Still he listened.

Then he heard it.

The buzzing drone of a locust. Then the whistling whoop of the bull bat. At last, the raucous bark of a coyote.

He was still attuned to the desert.

He was still alive.

But was that the paramount thing, mere living? He remembered what the old doc back in Yuma Prison had always told him. "To be or not to be, that is the question." Once he had asked the old man what those lines meant. The old geezer had explained that the lines asked whether it is better to live or to die. Slater had thought he knew the answer to that one until the old man had offered a third possibility.

"Perchance to dream."

He had Slater there. Slater had to admit that if a man could dream his way through life, without thirst or fear or pain or despair, what a wonderful thing it would be.

Slater had to smile at the thought, a smile of cracked, blood-caked, blistered lips, of a man broken on a blazing crucifix, spread-eagled in a barren desert pass, crushed under hell's own hammerblows.

But still it was a smile.

Then came the sickening realization of where his dream would end. Followed to its logical conclusion, he would die in this dream, faceless, nameless, his bare bones picked clean by ants, maggots, and vultures.

He shuddered violently. For one infinite heartbeat of eternity he feared he was going mad. He grabbed furiously at anything he could hold on to. "Though I walk through the valley of the shadow of death I shall fear no evil for... for... for..."

He remembered no more of the verse—and anyway those were just words. So instead he reached out for the memories of those whom he'd loved. Men like Bill Hickok and Cody. Women like Ghost Owl and Medea. And Cochise. Cochise.

At the mere thought of the man he felt solace. He wondered what Cochise would have done in a time like this. Slowly, his brain ceased to reel and his thoughts became lucid and focused.

He knew instantly what Cochise would have said: You cannot alter life. You cannot change things as they are or as they are to be. Cochise would have said that the man who knew other men's hearts certainly knew of life, but the man who knew his own soul knew the gods.

Suddenly, Slater knew what had to be done, what Cochise would have advised. He would achieve a martial mentality. He would clear his mind of everything but war. All softness, weakness, and fear of pain or blindness from the sun or loss of sanity or death would be banished. The point of this exercise was not to achieve power over nature or his enemies but over himself. If he was lucky, he might attain a sacred vision, the sort of vision that Cochise believed made all life's torments bearable, the sort of vision that brings peace to the mind, harmony to the heart, and solace to the soul.

With a light heart Slater rested on the desert floor. He no longer fought the restraining stakes and their rawhide thongs. Suddenly, it all seemed astonishingly simple. The desert, the great white swath of stars overhead, the heat and pain, even men like Sutherland and Flynn were as nothing— empty and void, as meaningless to Slater as were the Martian moons.

He lay back and stared peacefully at the stars overhead, his eyes glazed, his mind blank.

28

At noon the next day, when the sun was at its zenith, though Slater's mind was still blank, he was alert.

It was then that Cochise—or his instincts, or nature, or fate, call it what you will—told him to open his eyes.

And he saw the puma.

At first, he thought his vision had betrayed him and he was again insane. What was a panther doing so far into the desert? What did the big tom have to do with his martial mentality, his harmonious soul?

Then he realized this was no dream. What he was facing was reality, not the wisdom of the gods. The cat was, in fact, studying him coldly with calm, amber eyes, empty of all expression or emotion.

And he knew then that what the cat was so scrupulously studying was his next meal.

29

The shock of moving from a state of grace to a hellish inferno was devastating. When the cat jolted him back into the abyss it was as though he'd been kicked by a government mule.

An arch has but one keystone, and so does a man's sanity. Slater felt that keystone slipping once more.

Then he realized that he was now beyond madness.

His eyes stared straight into the sun.

The impact of the incredible desert heat struck him full force. His body seemed one vast, suppurating sore, and he could no longer shut his eyes. Under his convulsively twitching lids, his blood-streaked pupils viewed the world in a red glaring haze. The superheated air seared his lungs. A vise was slowly cracking his ribcage. His breath was the very breath of hell, pumping the air out of his body in short sobbing gasps.

Suddenly he caught a blur of real motion. He fought off pain and insanity, and his vision focused on the leaping thing.

The cat.

He leaped off a massive barn-sized boulder fifty feet to his left, in a tremendous parabolic jump. He could see him starkly now—a great slinky tom, long of body, massive of chest, reddish tan in hue, five full feet from nose to ass. He even noted that the flanks were speckled and shaded charcoal gray and that the head was astonishingly small for such a large body.

But the thing that struck Slater most was the tail. Long and lithe, curled and snaky, it stretched a good four feet, almost as long as the torso, and switched back and forth constantly. Meanwhile, the yellowish eyes remained dead-still in their empty, expressionless stare, unfathomable as God.

The cat walked slowly toward him.

Now Slater knew he was going to die. He lay there twitching, shattered and scourged. He was destroyed both physically and mentally, weighed in the balance and found wanting. He was possessed by an inconceivable fatigue. He knew now he had found his limit, not at the brink of hell's abyss but in the pit itself, a bottomless sink from which he would never return.

He had seen cats kill before. Indeed, he himself had once flushed a puma onto a scalphunting gunman in the Sonora desert. He had watched in awe, dread, and horror as the puma, shot smack through the heart, still found the strength to slash the man to ribbons and disembowel him like a slaughterhouse hog.

To be ripped and gutted by a panther—that was as bad a way to go as Slater had ever seen.

The agonized death mask on the victim's face had been grotesque beyond comprehension. He had truly been a man who gazed on the naked face of Satan before he died.

Now the cat was near, his shoulders dropping and sloping with each step, his rasping breath—*hrrrrh! hrrrrh! hrrrrh!*—filling the canyon. On and on he walked, closer and closer, till he was directly over Slater's chest, his scratchy, grating respiration almost deafening. Then his feline mask was directly over Slater's face. A long arching whisker casually brushed Slater's cheek, and as it did, Slater felt his bladder and bowels loosen. The cat's breath was unimaginably foul, and bile rose in Slater's gorge.

Then, to Slater's undying dismay, the puma began to lick his face. Not in the manner that a dog might lick his master—soft, soothing, gentle—but the way a file rasps a horseshoe.

Slater could not believe it was happening, but the pain struck with such searing clarity that he had to believe. The cat's tongue scraped and scraped his split, gnarled, festering lips and nose, no doubt for the salt.

Then he went to the open bleeding sores around the cheeks and eyes.

If Slater was ever to question a past in which violence and suffering had been the very stuff of his existence, this should have been the moment. The fetid breath, the rasping tongue, the heart-wrenching shock of the panther opening his bleeding sores...If ever Slater was to be sorry for his sins and crimes, the time had come.

At this moment he felt like a dying animal on the rack of an eternal hell, an insane thing, back arched like a bent bow, pain-maddened and terror-twisted, contorted crazily in the last throes of crucifixion.

He was almost ready to cry out to the God in Whom he'd never believed.

Just as Slater felt he had reached bottom, that he could go no lower in pain and despair, it got worse.

Much worse.

Slowly, with infinite, crucifying lassitude, the rasping tongue began to tear and scratch its way down every inch of his raw, bleeding body.

PART IX

30

Bear Dog lumbered slowly up the canyon. He was hot, hungry, thirsty, and tired. For the first time since the hunt had begun, he believed it possible that he would not catch the puma.

He'd started ten days before, with the old Mexican horse rancher and his son and daughter, the family who had taken him in after his mauling in the gaming pit.

But the humans couldn't take it.

Their horses had suffered in the heat. Then the food had given out. Then the water. In the end they had turned back. They had tried to make him come home with them, but there was no way. He'd kept on alone.

He wanted the cat too much.

For six straight days, Bear Dog had tracked the cat alone. The work was hot, hard, and dangerous. This was sparce, barren land for a dog with a powerful thirst and a big appetite. What little game he might have caught and devoured, the big panther had reduced to gnawed, cracked bones by the time Bear Dog arrived.

For the last two days Bear Dog had sunk to living off lizards, locusts, and an occasional desiccated bone. His hunger was as keen as any he'd ever know, and this was now more than a revenge hunt to Bear Dog. He had to kill and eat for his own nourishment. If he did not get a decent meal in his belly, he would never survive the return trek.

The panther had eliminated all the game on their backtrail.

He lumbered along on hot pads, thirst burning in his throat like fire, but his eyes alert, determined, concentrated. He was closing in on the big tom. He could feel it in his bones.

How Bear Dog had gotten himself into this fix he never really considered. It was his job. That was all. He had taken it on after that last, disastrous mauling down in the gaming pit. Afterward he'd come out of a three-day coma to discover himself the patient of a young Mexican girl. He was too sick to move or feed himself, so she had force-fed him a soft paste of ground meat, milk, and cornmeal; had dressed his deeply raked sides; and, when he was well enough to stay outside, she had taken him to the open-air mesquite-pole ramada and sat with him, his muzzle resting in her lap.

Bear Dog had found a new pack leader.

However, she was different from the other humans he had known. She was soft and gentle. In fact, too much so. She had the disconcerting habit of scratching and rubbing him behind the ears, of stroking and caressing his fur. Even worse, she frequently made soft cooing noises, which he despised.

Still, he managed to endure this fondling with a minimum of low-throated growls.

Bear Dog liked his new job well enough. He did not have to battle monster javelinas or boar grizzlies in a gaming pit. Not once had she, the old man, or the son attempted to whip him, something one or two previous leaders had mistakenly tried. The food was also good, even though it was mostly cooked and lacked the rough chewy texture of fresh-killed game. His only serious complaint was that it was too quiet. There were no local dogs to fight and kill, no bitches to fuck. They were too isolated.

They had only one basic employment for him, and Bear Dog took it up with alacrity. The horse ranch, having the only serious supply of fresh meat in that hard, bare desert country, was beset by prowlers. Coyotes and pumas often came down from the rimrock to attack the chickens, stock, and smokehouse. It was Bear Dog's job to keep these predators away. When occasionally he failed, the next morning the old man would take him to the scene of the crime, show him the interloper's tracks, and send him out after the thief. Frequently, the old man or his son would follow Bear Dog, but just as often they let him sniff the tracks, take off on his own, and return later in the day with the prowler's blood and fur crusted on his muzzle.

All in all, it was a good job, if a little slow, and Bear Dog had done well.

Until the puma arrived.

The big tom was the one chicken-stealing, colt-killing, smokehouse-raiding beast that he could not bring to bay and pull down, and it sometimes seemed to Bear Dog that the panther had come solely to torment him.

The cat was too stealthy and cunning, too strong and fast. When he invaded the ranch yard on his nightly jaunts, it was as if he were invisible, magically cloaked in the wings of night.

Even worse, the tom was not the standard hit-and-run thief, who violated the spread one or two nights and then moved on. As embarrassing as such a failure might have been, Bear Dog could have endured an occasional defeat. For instance, even after losing the colt that first night, Bear Dog was angry, but he could have lived with it. After the second night, when the cat had sneaked into the chicken house and devoured the two prize pullets, it would have been hard on the dog's vast pride, but he could have borne it. The third night, however, after a vastly successful raid on the smokehouse and the loss of a full quarter of good yearling beef, it was intolerable. The cat was not about to leave. Bear Dog would have to track and track and track the tom, as far as the panther might run, till he killed the cat—or the puma killed him.

There was no other choice.

31

Slater lay at the bottom of the canyon, a dying man in a dying gorge in a dying world. He knew now that what lay before him was not the end of waiting but the end of living. It was equally clear that the panther was fully fed and saving Slater for a later meal.

When he had licked Slater with his rasping tongue, he'd merely been playing with him.

Nonetheless, it had been terrible play. And while Slater believed he could bear almost any physical pain, this torture had been hard. After the cat had finished savaging Slater with his rasping tongue, Slater no longer experienced finite, quantifiable discomfort but a whole roaring ocean of suffering.

He knew now that some pain was beyond bearing.

He moved his head a fraction on an inch to the right, which was all the stakes allowed him, and looked up at the cat. The animal continued to stare down at him in rapt absorption with the same expressionless amber eyes. The tom was silhouetted against the breathless purity of the

bright turquoise sky, his breath rasping its
hrrrrh! hrrrrh! hrrrrh!

Beyond the cat, a hawk, heedless and free,
wheeled over the arroyo's rim, a diamondback
dangling in its talons. He watched as the hawk
released the rattler, let it drop to its death on
the rocks below, then dived to retrieve it.

Slater thought with crushing sadness that he
would have gladly traded places with the snake.

32

Toward dusk the ants came for him.

For two days he had sustained insect bites
from random flies, ants, and one droning bee-
tle. He had not even counted them as part of
the torture, dismissing them as inconsequential.

But no more.

Nearly a thousand red fire ants streamed up
his left leg with excruciating lassitude, pausing
here and there to sample the bloody provender.
Their travels produced unbearable itching, and
the bites, now at least a hundred a second,
blazed like balefire.

Even worse, beyond his feet Slater could see a
crimson river of ants. They were twisting toward him from several hundred feet up the

arroyo, from some remote anthill far beyond the canyon's winding bend.

He tried to cry out in his despair, but it hurt too much. His breath was a throat-scorched, lung-racking torture, and his stifled sobs rasped and rattled in his throat.

Again he glanced up at the big tom, straining his neck. He offered a silent prayer to the cat for a deadly deliverance from the ants.

He knew now with sickening certainty that these days in the canyon were not of this earth but on loan from hell.

33

Bear Dog cautiously approached the hard right-angle bend down-canyon. The scent of the cat was pungent and dense, almost omnipresent. He knew the puma could be anyplace, even stalking him. He was utterly aware of his own imminent danger.

Another smell flooded his nostrils. It was a man smell, but riper, more the smell of a human corpse, perhaps of a man dying. Mixed in with the cat scent, it was hard to identify, but something about the odor was stunningly familiar.

With extreme care Bear Dog started around the bend.

When he saw the tom.

He could not believe his eyes. The tom was on a huge high rock with his back to Bear Dog, staring at something in rapt fascination.

Slowly, silently, Bear Dog worked his way toward the cat, keeping himself between boulders. He sneaked a look at the thing the cat was studying so scrupulously.

A man staked out on the canyon floor like a green hide. The sun had more than scorched his body; it had left his naked carcass shredded, bleeding, and raw. Moreover, a seemingly endless queue of ants streamed toward him in a twisting scarlet trail.

Something gnawed at Bear Dog.

He knew this man, knew the smell, and though the body was burned virtually beyond recognition, he knew the eyes. That was it, the eyes. They were astonishingly black, flat as a Gila monster's.

He knew where he had seen those eyes and smelled that scent.

Lying under the grizzly, his life all but crushed out of him, through blood-dimmed eyes Bear Dog had seen the dead griz lifted. Then a man had pulled him out from under the bear and placed him on some boards. Later, when he was being hauled out of the pit, he'd forced his eyes open a second time, and the man had been straddling him, looking down at him with those amazing eyes.

Now Bear Dog glanced up at the tom. The puma was stiffening, heaving back on his haunches, preparing to spring.

The tom was planning to pounce on, slaughter, and devour the man who'd saved Bear Dog from the grizzly.

The big cat, which had decimated his leader's stock and outraged Bear Dog's pride, was about to kill Bear Dog's savior and rescuer, his...his... ...his friend.

All of Bear Dog's bloodlust welled up in him like hellfire. The fur along his back and across his shoulders bristled in waves, and his ears pressed flat against his head. His lips curled over the fangs in a silent snarl, and his eyes blazed. He heaved back on his own haunches, prepared for his own leap.

The tom wanted to kill his friend?

Bear Dog would have something to say about that.

34

From the canyon floor, Slater saw the tom—which two hours ago had returned to the boulder—stiffen.

And throw back his head.

Then he heard the bloodcurdling roar.

So that was that.

The end of waiting—and living.

It had come to this.

He braced for the cat's attack.

Then he saw the dog.

At first he could not believe his eyes. There he was, the big black beast that looked part wolf but mostly bear. The dog was staring at the cat, planning his attack.

Slater was at last convinced that he was losing his mind. He struggled to blot out the hallucination, but the vision of the huge black hound would not go away.

Abruptly a stream of fire ants reached his balls. The pain was massive.

He was convulsed by an explosion of agony sufficient to expunge even the most stubborn hallucination.

But the pain did not dim his vision of the dog.

Again Slater glanced up at the tom. The big cat was tensed for the kill. His tail twitched and snaked across the top of the boulder. Again he lifted his head and roared.

He heaved back on his haunches one last time and sprang.

35

Once more, the puma arced off the boulder in a long, high parabola, this time going straight for Slater.

He saw each bared fang, each arched talon with sickening clarity.

Then Bear Dog sprang.

He catapulted straight into the big tom like a cannonball a mere ten feet above Slater's spread-eagled body. He hit the tom laterally, his massive jaws catching the panther in the side of his snaky neck, clamping hard.

When Bear Dog struck, the big cat detonated. If before Slater had gaped at each flashing fang and talon, now he gaped as they turned on the hound. The tom's neck twisted at a grotesquely skewed angle as he writhed wildly in the dog's jaws. He was striving to twist in on Bear Dog, to face the hound and to drive his hind claws into the dog's belly.

But Bear Dog also fought. He kept his jaws locked on the side of the tom's neck as he straddled the cat's back and side, eluding the talons.

That was how it went. The cat twisting toward Bear's belly, back-arched and bristling, the dog spinning away from the claws. Turning in a clockwise direction at high speed, their flashing movements were little more than a blur. Twice they spun a full circle during their ten-foot fall.

The two animals landed skidding just below Slater's right shoulder. They struck with the force of their combined weight, four hundred pounds in all, propelled by the momentum of their tremendous jump and the centrifugal force of their whirling bodies.

Which was how they hit the stakes—laterally, with maximal impact.

And kept right on going.

They snapped one stake like breaking a pencil and ripped the other straight out of the arroyo hardpan in one stupendous burst.

Suddenly Slater's right hand was free.

He tried to move the arm, but strain on his constricted muscles and the sickening shock of his returning circulation was paralyzing, as exquisite an agony as any he had ever endured.

Even so, he felt the shock only with fleeting awareness. What held his concentration were the two rolling beasts. The one a tawny killer come down from the rimrock to feed on him, the other a great black hound, which he recognized as the dog he had saved from the pit.

A dog who had the heart to kill a boar grizzly.

If before Slater had lingered on the rack of an eternal hell, now he was aroused. It was as if all the iron in his backbone and all the fire blazing in his blood were pulling together for one last show of strength. If before he'd been crushed by the hammerblows of despair, now he was inspired and lifted up.

The floating sea of pain that undulated through his body was overwhelming, but still he reached for the foot-and-a-half-long stake with the needle-sharp point. The excruciating torment that each movement of his newly freed right arm evoked was paralyzing.

But still he did it.

He willed himself to move the arm, to grab the stake, to drag it toward him.

Slowly, an inch at a time, all but crucified by his returning circulation, he pulled at the stake.

He was not a moment too soon. The impossibly

overmatched Bear Dog was doing badly against the cat. He had hit the puma head-on, hoping to break his neck or at least stun him enough to turn him over and tear out his throat.

But he had failed.

This was one huge tom, by far the biggest Bear Dog had ever seen, let alone fought. The cat was not stunned, but had reacted to Bear Dog's attack with devastating savagery, not missing a beat.

Bear Dog now held a tiger, not by the tail, but by the side of the neck.

A grip he was losing fast.

And it wasn't much of a grip to begin with. Not when you considered how little it slowed down the panther, for the big cat moiled, twisted, and kicked even more violently.

If before their thrashing battle had dragged the pair away from Slater, now they spun back toward him. Less than a foot from Slater's right armpit, the whirling beasts stopped. Slater watched in horror as the big tom arched and twisted his back toward the ground, fighting to get his hind legs up under Bear Dog's belly.

My God, Slater thought, the cat is fast. It was common knowledge among the Apache that a puma's paws were quick enough to deflect an arrow in full flight, and that if you were ever wrestled to the ground and the cat got his hind legs underneath you, his back pressed against the earth, you were finished.

Nothing could stop those lightninglike talons from gutting you like a hog.

Slater squeezed the freed stake, and through

a blinding, searing sea of pain, he pulled it toward him.

The agony was exquisite. There Slater lay. The cat, which sought to torture and kill him, and the dog, which had leaped out of the blue to save his hide, were battling directly beside him.

But there Slater lay, stretched on a rack of convulsive crucifixion, each nerve in his right arm a scorching hellfire.

Still he did it.

He willed himself to retrieve the stake.

The cat was almost under the dog. He was already doing fearful damage to Bear's under-belly, raking it with great crimson slashes. Slater knew it would be only seconds before he gutted him.

With every ounce of strength, with every nerve in his body screaming against the pain, Slater lifted the stake over his head.

At that instant, the cat broke Bear Dog's grip, twisted the rest of the way under his belly, and unsheathed the arched hind claws.

Through his scorched mouth and throat, Slater roared in rage and pain. Rasping sobs racked his seared lungs. His heart hammered against his rib cage like a Gatling.

He drove the pointed stake home.

Straight through the puma's heart.

The panther's death scream crescendoed up and down the slickrock canyons. And at that precise moment Bear Dog tore out the vulnerable throat. With one lunge, he got both the jugular vein and carotid artery. In seconds the desert sand was awash with the puma's blood.

Torn Slater—stake still locked in his fist, the dead, exsanguinated puma beside him—blacked out.

And all his awareness vanished into the void.

36

Twice during the afternoon Slater came to.

The first time he was surprised to feel relatively numb below the waist. Maybe the fire ants had stripped his legs to the bone. He finally forced himself to look.

Bear Dog was cleaning the ants off his legs with broad wet strokes of his tongue.

Slater slowly looked to his right and left. The puma's carcass was no longer beside him. For a moment he feared the whole episode had been an insane hallucination.

Then he noticed the wide mop-streak of blood leading across the canyon.

Bear Dog had dragged the carcass of the cat directly into the path of the ants.

Now diverted from Slater's body, the ants were stripping the puma to the bone.

When he came to a second time, it was dusk.

HELL HOUND

The sun flared, then burst into a blood-red blaze over the rim of the arroyo, sending out dazzling streaks of yellow and red, violet and orange. It sank beneath the wall and was gone. The west wall cast its cool shadow over Slater.

He glanced down and saw Bear at his feet, protecting him from the few remaining fire ants with an occasional flick of his tongue. Bear Dog turned his head and met Slater's gaze. Slater found himself peering into the same sleepy, dreamy eyes that he had stared into that afternoon in the Comanchero gaming pit.

Slowly the dog rose. He lumbered up to Slater's head and stood there straddling his chest, as Slater had straddled his when he hauled him out of the pit. Bear Dog gave him a close look, his eyes blank and expressionless, empty, void.

The hound turned, walked back near Slater's feet, and lay down.

Bear Dog continued his vigil over Slater and the ants.

PART X

37

Shortly after the puma's death cry, Bear Dog heard the first three-shot volley.

He had not believed that the old man, the daughter, and the son could make it this far. They had started out with him on the puma's trail, but the mules did not have the bottom.

He thought they'd turned back for good.

He was wrong.

Still, they were not out of the cane. First, he had to do something about those ants, and after that there were those livid, lowering, anvil-shaped thunderheads to the west. If the storm clouds got to him and his stricken friend before they could escape, the gorge would be flooded, and they would drown.

Bear Dog had seen flash floods before. He had stood in *arroyos secos,* in dry washes, waterless as sun-bleached bones, the sun glaringly bright, with only the buzz of flies and the drone of locusts for company. Then suddenly it began. You would feel a strange trembling in the air and in the gorge. You would look up and see a mountain of water—dense, opaque, and in red-clay canyons often red as blood—thundering through the wash like a runaway locomotive on a downhill grade.

He looked at his friend and thought of the old man, the son, and the daughter.

Would they get here with ropes and mules to pull them out?

Or would the flash flood get to them first?

38

When Slater came to, it was unusually dark. Since in the cloudless purity of the desert sky the stars glitter with dazzling brilliance and the Milky Way is a broad swath of white light, something was clearly wrong.

Slater glanced down at his feet. In the dark, he saw Bear Dog stir. The dog got up from his vigil and trotted over to his face. He licked it once, then trotted up-canyon. He looked over his shoulder as if urging him to follow.

Slater agreed it was a good idea, but right now he just wasn't up to it.

Bear Dog returned.

Gradually, as Slater's eyes became more accustomed to the night, he recognized the problem. Massive inky clouds had filled the sky, eclipsing the moon and stars. In the distance he heard the high whining shriek of storm winds, and to the west, above the rim of the canyon, sheet lightning blazed.

Instantly Slater understood.

Slowly, with excruciating effort, he struggled to bring circulation back into his limbs. His right hand freed, he attempted to untie one-handed the hard tight knot that held his neck thong.

The dog came over and quickly chewed apart the thong.

The pain of movement was so severe that it took him the better part of an hour, even with Bear Dog's help, to free himself from the stakes. Even at that, he was not much better off. His body was a mass of second- and third-degree burns, he was stark naked, and he was not able even to crawl, let alone walk.

And then he felt it.

Great tentative raindrops slapped his face, throat, and crotch. His first reaction was to throw back his head and open his mouth to the rain, but then, over the rim of the canyon, thunder growled and sheet lightning blazed.

He knew he had to escape the gorge.

He glanced at Bear Dog. The animal's eyes were still and expressionless, yet he knew the dog understood.

As he struggled to sit up, the rain came down in slanted, layered sheets, sweeping the length and breadth of the canyon. Each movement for Slater was torturous, but despite the agony, the rain, the rumbling thunder, and the blazing sheet lightning, curiously enough, with the big dog at his side, Slater was hopeful.

He pulled himself up and started for some small boulders strewn along the wall of the gorge. He was almost paralyzed with pain, but still he reached them. When Bear Dog started up the scree-strewn slope, Slater grabbed his fur and let himself be half-pulled, half-carried up the incline.

Now the drumfire rain was tumultuous, and for a moment Slater felt as if he were lying under a waterfall. The boulders were slippery and the footing was bad. Bear Dog was skidding on the wet rock as they made their ascent. Slater spread himself out on Bear Dog's back and hung on to the storm-soaked, furry shoulders.

The wind ululated high above the hammering of the rain. Slater felt the water crashing over his neck and shoulders. He struggled in agony up the slippery slope through a night as black as the abyss.

Then he felt it—the weird, almost volcanic rumbling—and when he looked up-canyon, he certainly sensed it, even if he did not see it at first.

It was coming straight at them.

Rim-high and tight against the walls, the flash flood looked not so much like a river but a mountainous tidal wave of water.

Hurtling at them at high speed.

They never had a prayer of getting out of its path.

With Slater still clutching Bear Dog's shoulders, the flash flood picked the two of them off the arroyo wall and swept them back into the abyss.

PART XI

PART II

39

Perchance to dream, the old Yuma Prison doctor had told Slater so many years ago. And for a long time that is what he did.

In a coma for three weeks, he had little else to do.

And dream he did.

He dreamed often and long of the female Apache war shaman whom he'd once loved and whom he had watched tumble head over heels to a fiery death. When his memories of the life they might have had were too painfully shadowed by her death, his dreams moved on.

He relived the period when he'd languished in the hell of Yuma Prison. He dreamed of Bill Hickok and Calamity Jane, how they had appeared to him like bolts from the blue, and how they had not only arranged his escape but helped him even a score with Coleman Younger.

But those dreams, too, were marred. Hickok slept in an unquiet grave on Mount Moriah in the Dakota territory, the victim of failing eyes, too much fame, and a paid assassin's bullet.

And Slater had not been there to help.

Calamity? She was back to her old trade, hustling drinks and tricks in an El Paso brothel.

And he'd never even had the grace to visit her there, let alone offer a helping hand.

His dreams drifted endlessly. Sometimes he recalled those three long years in the Sonoran Pit, shackled to Raphael Marquez, perhaps the best friend he'd ever had. This was a man who had not only helped to keep him alive in the worst prison hellhole on earth, but had saved Slater's sanity and planned their escape.

And what had he done for Marquez? When Marquez lay dying with a chest full of lead and a mouth full of blood, Slater, against his friend's will, had administered the coup de grace.

And then had made good his escape.

And what of Dolores, the woman who had given her life to rescue both him and Marquez from the Sonoran Pit? She was the woman he had vowed to marry, but instead she had fallen prey to the torture squads of Diaz and that bastard Sutherland.

He remembered how once during an "interrogation session" of his own, Diaz had asked, "Why are you so tough? Your friends, after I get through with them, they are not tough at all. They are dead."

Slater had given Diaz his usual *hombre-duro* answer: "Maybe I need tougher friends."

But the truth was much different.

His friends had been tougher than government mules. They'd all had more guts than you could hang on fifty miles of line fence, every one of them harder than Arkansas bedrock.

Their problem had been their loyalty to Slater.
That was what had done them in.

Or at the very least, his failure to be there
when *they* needed him.

Hickok, Calamity, Doc Harper, Ghost Owl,
Medea, Marquez, all.

Flynn, back there in the canyon, had summed
it up.

Slater was weighed in the balance and found
wanting.

40

When Slater finally came to, it was night. He
was lying on a feather tick in an adobe farm-
house. A pretty young Mexican woman was
sitting in a chair alongside his bed.

He was covered head to foot with neat's-foot
oil.

Like a soaped saddle.

He tried to lift his head, and in that instant
he heard the soft padding of four feet. They
came up alongside the bed and stopped in front
of the girl.

It was the largest, blackest hound he'd ever
seen.

Bear Dog.

The hound put his muzzle over the edge of the bed, and the woman opened her eyes. Both she and the dog stared at him. He opened his mouth to speak, but his breath rasped and rattled in his throat.

The woman gave him a clay cup filled with cool water. She held it up to his mouth, and he drank.

"Where . . . ?" he finally croaked out.

"Shhh," she said, placing a finger to her lips. "Bear Dog found you in the canyon. We had been tracking a puma that had decimated our stock, and in the process—apparently after killing the panther—Bear Dog found you."

"The flood?" Again the words croaked in his throat.

"He pulled you out of the flash flood."

Slater shut his eyes.

"I'm not sure if you remember us," the girl went on. "You and some amigos stopped by our ranchero one afternoon with a very sick dog. We nursed him back to health, and he has been with us ever since. But he still remembers you and looks after you. He never leaves your room. Whatever the tie is, it is strong."

Slater nodded slowly.

"How do you feel?"

"Hurt," he said.

"Yes, you've drifted in and out of consciousness for three weeks, but you're better now. You've healed quickly. The front half of your body, it was scorched *muy malo*," very bad. *"De veras,"* in truth, "the family never thought you would make it."

He said nothing.

"I know. It must be hard, but try to be still. Really, the burns and sores are almost healed. It's only a matter of time before you're well."

"Why...?" he barely choked the word out, but still she caught his meaning.

"Do not worry. You are in Christ's house. In this dwelling we are all God's children. In fact, I am to be a bride of Christ. A nun. Soon. I'm home to look after a few things. So you have nothing to fear. This is a devout family. When a man is rescued from the flood as you were and left to our care, we consider it God's work. For some reason He chose to deposit you with this family, and we shall do His bidding. I do not know what that may be. When we met you that first time, you were with, well, some very unsavory men, but things are different now. My father and I are convinced that this is God's doing."

Slater stared at the ceiling. His dreams were still vivid, and he remembered all the harm he had brought his friends. He would bring this family no good. He knew it in his heart. The only hope for them was for him to leave as soon as possible.

She raised the cup to his mouth, and he drank.

He would need his strength.

He had to leave for their sakes.

As soon as he could mount a horse.

41

For the next three days Slater's throat was swollen shut, and he had to fight for every breath. He spent most of his waking hours outdoors under the maguey-thatched ramada. He drowsed in the cool shade on a Navajo blanket. Bear Dog was constantly at his side, his muzzle resting on crossed paws, not letting his leader out of sight.

Slater's body was tight and itchy from the healing of the burns, and the woman named Madelina daubed it with neat's-foot oil. His head was swathed in bandages. His left arm, broken near the bicep, was splinted. The splint was secured with clean rags on each side of the break. The wrist hung from a neck sling.

Slater studied the small spread while his throat and body healed. He knew it was in a subdesert of the Great Chihuahua Shelf, and it looked to be a pretty hungry proposition. A few wind-scoured corn patches with chilis and pinto beans planted between the rows, a little maguey, and a patch of diamondback melons. A few head of steer, a dozen chickens, the scent of fresh broom sage.

But they had a remuda that was worth some money. It took a long time to build a string like that. It was obvious from the looks of the stock corral that the old man had had a blooded stud at one time. Slater could see that from all the long legs and white knee-high stockings. There was a nice steel-dust gelding. Over there, a beautiful roan pony. The old man had a colorful assortment of good-looking duns and bays, a handsome buckskin, a rangy-looking palomino, and one spectacular Appaloosa.

Yes, the old man knew horses. You might guess that from the drooping, solemn mustache, or from the deeply etched wind-squint around the eyes, or from the brown *indio puro* skin burned dark as old leather by the llano sun.

But mostly you could read horse sense in his knuckle-popped, rope-scarred hands. One look at those and you knew he was a wrangler.

Slater glanced around him at the four-room adobe shack. A nice old Spanish arch over the doorway, a few good pieces of furniture, crucifixes on every wall.

He looked up and saw the girl. Seventeen, he guessed, eighteen tops. She was dressed to the chin in one of those white *peón* blouses and wore several layers of skirts, down to her ankles. Her two wrist-thick braids glistened black as obsidian and, even though they were densely plaited, hung halfway down her back. She had wide flaring cheekbones and dark almond-shaped eyes, which always seemed to stare at him quizzically, as if confused. She was not nearly as dark as her father, and her nose was aquiline.

Apparently she'd had a gringa mother. Her eyes seemed more than a little distant. Nonetheless, frequently she poured him cups of cool well water, and encouraged him to drink the rich, nutritious pinole, a dense mixture of cornmeal, ground mesquite beans, and water.

Now his throat was no longer swollen, and when she handed him his cup, he said, "*Muchas gracias.* The water's good."

"We have one spring-fed well. The rest, though is llano water."

"Meaning?"

"Meaning, amigo," her brother said, entering the ramada, "that the ground water is so hard you could hone an ax with it."

He stared out over the countryside. This was virgin llano, little more than wind-waved mesquite, broom sage, and bear grass.

"Why do you stay?" Slater asked.

"People leave us alone. All the other land has been taken up by the *haciendados* and the people forced into *peónage.* This desert llano, we get by on it, and we're safe. The land is so barren no one else desires it."

Slater nodded. "So you don't have any close neighbors?"

"None to handshake or speak to." It was the father who spoke. He had just stepped under the arbor.

"That is good," Slater said. "There are things you must know about me. Then, as soon as I can sit a horse, I must be gone from here. I can bring you great trouble. Terrible trouble."

The old man motioned the boy into the house.

He came back with a piece of paper ten inches wide and fifteen inches long.

"Do you know what this is? A man rode by a month ago handing them out."

Slater did not have to be told, but when the boy held it under his face, he glanced at it anyway. The first line read: REWARD: $20,000.

A rather bad likeness of his face followed, featuring a heavy mustache but minus the beard he'd favored since escaping from Sonora Prison.

The rest of the copy read:

OUTLAW TORN SLATER: WANTED IN 13 STATES AND TERRITORIES AND IN THE PROVINCES OF SONORA AND CHIHUAHUA.

CRIMES: *Bank-robbing, train robbing, mail theft, hijacking of arms and troop shipments, assault with intent to do bodily harm, assault with intent to kill, arson, kidnapping, malicious destruction of public property, escape from the Yuma and Sonora federal correctional institutions, supplying of arms to hostiles and bandidos, and assorted counts of murder-most-foul.*

DISTINGUISHING FEATURES: *Diagonal knife scar transversing torso from left groin to right shoulder, puckered bullet scar entering below right clavicle, exiting above shoulder blades. Back heavily scarified with broad white stripes of Yuma and Sonora prisons.*

WARNING: *Notorious knife specialist. Expert in all forms of small arms, munitions, and demolition. Is exceedingly dangerous. Under no circumstances attempt to subdue or apprehend.*

WANTED: Dead.

On the reverse side was printed the Spanish translation.

"Twenty thousand dollars is a lot of money," Slater said.

The old man stared at him. "We do not take blood money," he said.

Slater pointed to the poster.

The old man cut him off. "Do not fear. Though I may not approve of the way you earn your living, you will be safe here. Nobody will come to check."

"You don't know these people like I do."

"We shall discuss it after supper. Let your throat rest. Gather your strength. For three weeks you have been sleeping like the dead. Perhaps you died *uno poco*," a little.

"They will come to check."

"Be still. We shall talk later."

42

After supper the son, the daughter, and the old man sat around Slater's sickbed. The woman was still in her *peón* blouse and skirt but the men were without their big straw sombreros.

"What exactly happened?" Slater asked, addressing the father.

"We arrived at the canyon's rim just as the flash flood hit. You and the dog were attempting to scale the side of the gorge. You were clinging to him. The flood pulled both of you off, and you hung on."

"The dog pulled me out of the water?"

The old man nodded.

"What else?"

"The front of your body was badly burned. Your wrists and ankles were scarred with thong marks. You looked as if—"

"As if what?"

"As if you'd been staked out on the canyon floor, left to die from the ants and the heat."

"That's how they planned it."

"It is a bad way to die."

"They don't get much worse."

The old man nodded, and Slater looked around the room. Three people. Not one of them looked as if they'd ever cocked a Colt in anger.

And now his presence might buy them more trouble than they could ever handle.

"I don't mean to sound ungrateful, but I gotta be movin' on. You weren't supposed to save me. You were supposed to kill me. The wanted poster means just that. I don't think you appreciate the fix you're in."

"Amigo, we are a godly family, meaning we do not kill. Since God chose to deposit you in this household, He must have had a reason. We were called upon to keep you alive. We did just that."

"That act could be your funerals. With no magnolias or slow music neither."

"Amigo, we do not view you as trouble."

"Well, I'm sure glad I got rescued by you 'stead of, say, them 'Paches. I sure as hell needed more lookin' after than a couple of gourd rattles and an eagle-plumed medicine stick shook at me."

"Your medical care was the work of my daughter, Madelina," the old man said. "She worked at the convent last summer. She was trained as a nurse. She can splint bones, suture wounds, even deliver babies."

"My enemies catch up to you, might be handier if she slung a Colt."

"What need have we of a *pistola* around here?" asked Hernando, the old man's son. He looked to be around sixteen.

"Well, they're primo for killin'," Slater said. "Otherwise they don't count for much, I s'pose. You can do better with a hammer for poundin' nails."

"My friend, we like to consider this a house of the Lord. We do not advocate murder here."

"The men lookin' for me, they sure do. And they obviously don't believe I'm dead. Otherwise they wouldn't be puttin' out these handbills. When they come by here, they'll do more'n speak of murder."

"What sort of man are you, people want you dead so bad?" Madelina asked.

"I'm a man to ride the owlhoot with. That's all."

"What's that?"

"A rogue outlaw. A buck cut loose from the herd."

"And these men do not like that."

"They don't like nothin' 'cept bad women, worse whiskey, and what puts pesos in their pockets."

"They are killers?"

"They'd shoot stars if they saw 'em fall."

"And you think they shall come after you?"

"Let's call it my eternally suspicious nature."

"What you do not properly understand is that we are all God's children. Christ Jesus taught us to love our enemies."

"That may go in an insane asylum, but not Chihuahua."

"This little ranchero, amigo, is no insane asylum."

"Yeah, but it is in the middle of the Mexican desert, a million miles from nowhere. You just ain't known men like Diaz or Sutherland or them Comancheros."

"And how about men like you, señor?" Madelina asked. "That poster says you rob and murder. What is the difference between you and them?"

"I never robbed nobody poor as you. And with these kind of men, the poorer, gentler, and more helpless you are, the harder it'll go."

"Then we must convert them," Hernando said.

"How?"

"Through love, reason, and God's eternal grace."

"That may work on some men, but not on

no Comancheros. Only thing convert men like them's a floggin' post or a rack. A taut noose, a droppin' trapdoor, and God's mercy on their souls."

"How would they find us?" Hernando asked. "We live alone in the middle of the llano."

"Through informers. Men who are paid to rat out their friends or frightened not to. This land is filled with informers."

"Amigo," said Carlos, the old man, "I have listened carefully, but I cannot accept what you say. Christ's cross is burden enough in this world. I cannot yield to fear. Therein lies despair. And our Mother Church tells us that the only unforgivable sin is despair. That is so."

"Whatever you say. Still, I'm gonna be outa here come dawn."

"But your health?"

"It won't get no better if them Comancheros track me here."

"Amigo, you must learn to be more trusting."

"Oh, I trust all right. I trust in a headstart, a fast horse, and a red-hot navy Colt smokin' in my fist."

"You know, señor, I am truly glad you are going," Madelina said, "and these things my father says about your healing being the work of God, I am not so sure. What use could God possibly have for a man as unprincipled as you?"

"I got a code."

"Yes? And this code, given the way you live, is it for good or for evil?"

"It comes before good and evil. And after."

Her father gave her a harsh stare. "Madelina, do not judge this man. The Lord moves in mysterious ways. We only serve. Whatever Christ's purposes for any of us, that is His doing, not ours."

"Still, I say it anyway. I do not like this man. He is bloody-minded and sick to his soul. Death is his constant companion. You can see it in the way he walks, talks, in his very eyes. He says if he can mount a horse, he will be gone at dawn. So be it. And he can take that hound of hell with him, too, the one who saved him from the flood. Any man with a wanted poster such as that," she pointed to the dodger on the shelf, "does not deserve further help. Had I known who he was, I would have let him die."

Slater's smile was gentle. "Weren't there somethin' in the Bible 'bout Christ eatin' with thieves and publicans?"

"Yes," her father agreed, "and He was crucified with thieves, one of whom He forgave and to whom He granted eternal life."

"We are not Christ Jesus," Madelina argued.

"I thought you was fixin' to be His bride," Slater said.

"But not His whore."

Her father glared. "Such language from a daughter who would commit herself in Christ. All right. That is enough. Mr. Slater, if you think it wise, at dawn you shall have a good horse. As my daughter says, the dog goes too. He seems to have some special attachment to you, and you will need help. I can only pray that my daughter is wrong. Otherwise, may God have mercy on all our souls."

He motioned to his son and daughter to snuff the candles and the one coal-oil lamp. Then he turned toward his bedroom in the back of the ranchero.

43

At sunup Slater was dressed in *peón* clothes and a straw hat and mounted on a common, un-branded bay. He dallied the reins around the saddle horn. He lashed his hips to the cantle and horn with a length of lass rope, then strapped his wrists to it with a thong. He silently prayed he could stay on.

He kicked the horse and was off, heading south. Later he would double around and ride north, straight into the south Texas horn.

For a few seconds the dog followed him, then stopped and stared back at the farm, confused. Hernando flung a rock at Bear Dog and hit him in the rump.

The situation was clarified.

Bear Dog fell in beside the bay.

Bear Dog followed his leader.

The one who had saved him from the grizzly.

And the puma.

The one whom he had saved from the flood.

He matched the horse's stride with his tireless wolf's lope.

PART XII

44

Two dozen Comancheros lolled in their saddles
on the rim of a narrow canyon. Gentleman Jim
Flynn studied them carefully. The first one he
considered was their boss. Sutherland was a
dapper limey in a red bowler with a silver and
turquoise hatband. He wore a fresh ruffled
shirt of white shantung silk, the tails tucked into
purple whipcord jodhpurs. The dandified riding pants bloomed outrageously around the thighs
and tapered tightly against the knees. They
were carefully tucked into black thigh-high riding boots of imported calfskin. A black British
swagger stick was tucked under his arm. He was
smoking fruity-smelling tailor-mades. The intri-
cately carved teak cigarette holder was cocked
in his mouth at a jaunty angle.

The left half of Sutherland's scalp was a white
hairless swath of scar tissue.

A small token from a previous encounter with
Torn Slater.

Flynn's eyes rested more pleasantly on the
vivacious Judith McKillian.

She was sitting on a huge jet-black stallion nearly eighteen hands.

And she looked immaculate.

Her black-felt sombrero with elaborate gold and silver embroidery was somehow free of dust and sweat. The three-foot scoop brim, after four weeks on the trail, was still perfectly shaped. Her gossamer-sheer blouse of pongee silk was stretched tautly against her nipples and looked freshly laundered.

She wore it unbuttoned to the navel.

His gaze drifted downward. Below the waist, she was squeezed into a pair of astonishingly tight, red whipcord Levi's, the legs tucked into gleaming black knee-high riding boots. These were heeled with five-inch sterling silver buzzsaw rowels.

The rowels, as well as her four-foot double-plaited wrist quirt, were streaked with horse blood.

Slowly, luxuriatingly, Flynn's gaze traveled up the waist-length mane of flame-red hair tumbling casually over her shoulders and back. His gaze drifted up to her face, which he studied with meticulous care. He paused to consider the wide-set emerald eyes and flawless alabaster skin, the kind sometimes called buttermilk, which stretched tightly over wide, flaring cheekbones and yet left the generous lips looking soft and sensual.

She was so achingly, yearningly, heart-stoppingly beautiful that he wished he'd never seen her.

In one quick sweep Flynn took in the rest of that sorry lot.

Comancheros.

God, were they a filthy crew. Rank, hung-over, stinking of rotgut, dirt, and sweat, hunched over their saddles. Their eyes smoldered with violence or, when they looked on the McKillian woman, with obscene lust.

Flynn turned his eyes to Sutherland, who was complaining to Flaco.

"Look, my good man, I don't care how many times we canvass these canyons, the fact is we aren't finding him."

"Señor, you hear what the *peónes* say. There was flash floods in these here canyons, no? The man, he was staked out tight, tighter'n a gnat's fuckin' asshole, but he got ripped apart by the flood, no? He got lost and buried someplace. It happen that way sometimes. All right, I be *muy* sorry you no get to see his dead body. I be even more *muy* sorry that we don't get that bonus you promise when you see him all staked out. But, boss, there ain't nothin' we can do 'bout that now."

"The hell there isn't," Sutherland said.

Flaco glanced sideways at Flynn. "Eh, amigo, you explain it to him, huh? He no seem to *sabe*."

Flynn looked at Flaco a long moment. "No, my friend. This is something you no *sabe*. Let me be more specific. We do not leave Chihuahua till we find Slater's remains or some undeniable proof of his passing."

"What?" Flaco was baffled.

"It is imperative," Sutherland said, "that we verify the thing is dead. You know, find a stake through his heart. See him drawn, quartered, castrated. Watch him shot between the eyes with a silver fucking bullet. Personally, I would like to cremate his dismembered corpse and scatter the ashes over an erupting volcano."

"I no un'erstan'," Flaco said.

"Slater," Flynn said, "is a very hard man to kill, and his earthly demise should never be assumed, guessed at, or taken for granted. If we do not find Slater's unquiet grave and he is in fact alive, there will be hell to pay. I know. I've seen him in action. Mr. Sutherland has seen him in action. He is Satan's own scourge. If there is even one chance in hell he lives, we will follow his trackless trail till that one infernal chance freezes over. Mark my words. We cannot afford to be wrong about this. Any of us."

"So what do we do?" Flaco asked.

"We track and track and track. We interrogate *peónes* using the most persuasive means at our disposal. Then we track and track and track some more. Till we find that hell spawn, dead or alive."

"And if we don't find him?"

"Oh, we'll find him." Flynn said, "If he's above ground, dead or breathing or somewhere in between, we'll find him. Just as sure as shit stinks and buzzards eat carrion. And it's not for the bonus, either. We have to find him. If we have to harrow hell for his lost, tormented soul."

Flaco heaved a hard sigh. He ordered the gang to spread out along the rim of the canyon. As they began scouting the gorge, Flynn earnestly prayed they would cut Slater's sign.

45

A heavily scarred gringo in dirty frayed *peón*
clothes slumped in his saddle. He was riding a
common, unbranded bay. A huge black hound
lumbered through the water beside them. Slowly,
clumsily, the horse and the dog found the bottom. They clambered up the bank.

The mare was not in much better shape than
the gringo. Goose-rumped, cow-hocked, and
saddle-galled, she was nothing more than a rack
of bones. For six long weeks she'd lived off trail
graze sparce enough to starve ground squirrels.
She'd drunk wallow water that was so hard the
gringo could have flayed a slaughterhouse hog
in it without adding heat or lye.

But she'd endured.

And the gringo, living off the very same llano
water and off game chased down by the dog,
had survived.

He kicked the foundering mare up the Rio
Grande's north bank and onto the muddy path
along the shore. The sky was turning pale gray
with first light. He'd deliberately chosen the
slowest time of the day to enter El Paso. He

doubted anybody would recognize him, but still he tried to lower the odds.

The three continued downstream, the gringo searching with squinted eyes for the little island in the middle of the river known as Esmeraldo. It was one of those sand-pits neither country claimed.

Calamity Jane had built a saloon-brothel there.

Esmeraldo was literally beyond the law.

Esmeraldo was to be his home.

PART XIII

46

It was near dusk when the dapper limey and the beautiful red-haired lady, followed by the two dozen hired hardcases, rode into Carlos's ranch yard. Many weeks had passed since the gringo had left the small spread, heading south, intending to circle north.

Long ago Carlos had stopped thinking of the gringo's warnings.

So much time had passed.

Who could care anymore?

Carlos looked up at the strangers and grinned.

Even when the tall, dark-haired man in the solemn black mustache and black stovepipe hat rode forward and pinned him with those hard, mirthless eyes, Carlos grinned, naïvely secure. The man rode closer, and Carlos's smile widened. He even took off his hat and wrung it humbly in front of him, as *peónes* in the haciendas were taught to do. Now the man grinned as well, though Carlos wondered fleetingly why the grin never reached the man's eyes.

"You recognize this?" the man said, handing him a Torn Slater wanted poster.

Carlos stared at Slater's picture. Suddenly, he did not know what to do. Nervously, he shook his head no.

Now the grin reached the man's eyes. A wrist quirt whistled through the air, and Carlos's cheek burst into blood and flames, blinding his eyes with tears. The quirt whistled again, this time reversed. The shot-loaded butt stock came down hard, and Carlos's head exploded.

When he came to, he was sitting on the ground, his daughter, Madelina, holding his swollen, bloodied head.

"Recognize us now?" Flynn said.

Slowly Carlos's vision began to clear.

Flaco shouted, "Who you think I am? Father Christmas? The Tooth Fairy?"

Now Carlos recognized them.

Comancheros.

The same band that, when led by Slater, had brought him the dog.

Carlos looked at his family and began to sob.

They were in for their issue of big-time trouble.

47

As Madelina watched the Comancheros loot and search their house, she could not believe her eyes. The gold-plated rosary, the antique filigreed locket that contained their only portrait of her mother, her grandfather's key-winding Waltham pocket watch, the two bronze candlesticks—all were tossed outside the house onto the frayed Navajo blanket.

They did not own much, and the house was small. Soon the search came to an end. The last man to leave was the one they called Flaco. He confiscated three gallons of coal oil from out back and held a piece of folded parchment in his teeth.

Slater's wanted poster.

She'd forgotten that it was out by the woodpile under the tinder.

They'd all forgotten it.

Now they would pay.

She watched to her undying horror as her father's wrists were jerked behind his back and lashed together crosswise. She stared gape-jawed as Bloody Flaco and Lorenzo grabbed her father under the armpits and half-marched, half-dragged him across the dirt yard toward the big cottonwood with the long overhanging limb. By the time they reached the tree, her father's feet were dragging, and their chickens were flapping in six directions at once.

A blur of activity caught her eye. She glanced sideways. An old man with a long gray beard was tying off a thirteen-coil nooseknot. It was a good hemp rope. He tossed the lariat across the yard to Flynn.

Flynn held the knotted rope in one hand, paused to study it, then crossed the yard to

Madelina. When he was directly in front of her, he said calmly, a hint of brogue throbbing through his voice, "Now, child, I know you're a good girl, and you want to do the right thing. But this Mr. Slater, whom you people deny knowing, and yet whose picture you so obviously cherish, well, he's a very bad man. And unless you give us certain information as to his whereabouts, things will go hard for ye. Do you understand that?"

Madelina nodded.

"So I'm going to ask you just once, and please," he said, turning to her brother and father, "nobody be bashful. Speak up one and all, if you so wish. Tell me where the man is."

There was silence.

Flynn returned his gaze to Madelina. "Yes?"

"We do not know, señor."

"Well now, I might be willing to believe that, except that we have already caught your father in a very serious lie when he denied knowing Mr. Slater. And now we discover that you even keep this unflattering portrait of him around your ancestral acres. So you see why I'm a little hesitant to accept your word."

"We do not know where he is," she said softly.

"Perhaps, but you see now I need something concrete to convince me. An auto-da-fé, an act of faith, so to speak. Otherwise, how can I be sure you're speaking honestly?"

He turned and studied the old man and the son for a moment. "Flaco, get the boy. Put him against that cottonwood and shoot him."

Suddenly Madelina was sobbing. She blurted, "But we do not know where this Señor Slater is.

Truly. And my brother is but a boy, a child. He is so innocent."

The dapper Englishman in the red bowler, ruffled silk shirt, and outrageous jodhpurs trotted up to her on his big deep-chested gray. The horse whinnied and blew a long rolling snort. Sutherland patted the animal's neck.

"So much the better. Then his soul shall be stainless when he meets his maker."

"*Excelencia*," she cried, "what good does this heinous atrocity do?"

Sutherland's brow furrowed in derision. "My dear, I'm afraid that violence which you so subjectively condemn as a 'heinous atrocity,' I see, well, as heroism."

"Why?" her father, now seated on the hanging horse, shouted, "why us?"

"As the poster clearly states, Torn Slater is *Wanted: Dead*. When you helped Mr. Slater, you interfered with justice. My justice."

"Justice belongs to Christ Jesus," Madelina wailed.

Sutherland stared irritably at Flynn, who was still standing in front of the girl.

" 'Justice belongs to Christ Jesus'? I wish these *peónes* weren't so damnably clever. I despise cleverness in *peónes*. It suggests they don't know their place."

"We can't all be blooded aristocrats," Flynn observed.

"Thank God!" Sutherland said.

The boy in front of the tree was suddenly kicking and sobbing. Flaco held him there, while Lorenzo punched him twice in the face. The kid now bled from the nose and mouth, but still he fought. Flaco yelled across the yard, "Boss, what should we do with him?"

"I don't know. I fear that with all this damnable *peón* cleverness, these people shall need a lesson. A very painful lesson. Instruct him."

Lorenzo and Flaco slammed the boy backward into the tree, hard. The crack on the head stunned him momentarily, and he stopped struggling. Lorenzo's .45 flashed from the cross-draw holster, and he shot the boy three times in the chest. The rounds hit in rapid succession, *onetwothree,* so earsplitting in their intensity that they did not register as individual shots but as one protracted roar.

However, they did register visually.

Each shot picked the boy up and slammed his body into the cottonwood, the arms flailing and outflung, like those of a mad, demented marionette with the strings cut.

His body slid down the treetrunk, the arms and legs jerking convulsively.

Madelina collapsed at Flynn's feet, sobbing. He twisted her long braided hair tightly in his fist, three full turns, and, ripping open the front of her *peón* blouse with his other hand, jerked her violently to her knees. Flynn slapped her face hard, forehand and backhand. Without releasing his grip, he said softly:

"*Muchacha,* now you must give up Slater or the old man. You have but one choice, I'm afraid. Either/or. You can't have it both ways."

"We do not know."

"Then you and your father will die. Where you are. Slow and hard."

"There is nothing to tell."

"Please, little lady," Flynn said, his voice still soft, the faint hint of the lilting brogue still there, "if you mistakenly think my friends here to be genteel respecters of your stainless femininity, think again. There are no Sir Walter Raleighs here. No one will fling his cloak upon this rank and muddy puddle for you. I cannot let you harbor any such illusions."

"Señor, in Christ's name, let us go," her father moaned.

"You speak of Christ?" Sutherland said, his eyebrows arching with disdain. "Forget him. He's not here. I am. I alone stand between you and darkest night. Beyond me lies only the abyss."

"Please," she heard her father wail. "We are not savage apes in darkest Africa. We are human beings."

Sutherland glanced at Flynn, amused. "I hope they're not dumb enough to expect mercy from *me*."

"My curse will follow you to your grave," her father shrieked.

He began chanting Hail Marys, one after the other.

Flynn looked up at Sutherland. "I think we lost the old man."

"Not quite," Sutherland said, glancing around the ranch yard. His eyes fell on a bale of barbed wire over by the house. He nodded to it. "Use it on the bitch's face."

Flynn nodded to Flaco. He retrieved the ax

from the woodpile and chopped off a strip. He walked over to Flynn, who still held the girl kneeling before him, her long black hair twisted tightly in his fist. He wrenched her head back sharply till her face was staring straight up into the sky.

Flaco drove the barbed wire deep into her right cheek just below the ear. He dragged it diagonally down her face to the very tip of her chin, twisting and gouging the barbs. He left a long, jagged, bone-gaping trail, bloody and zigzagged.

Her father opened his eyes, stopped his incantation, and stared at his daughter in horror.

"Got your attention?" Sutherland asked. "Good. Because it doesn't end here. This stirring extravaganza will not close with your untimely death. If you hang with this dark secret still brooding in your soul, your daughter will suffer the tortures of hell. On that you have my word."

"But Madelina," he rasped, "she's to become a bride of Christ, pledged to Our Savior. She is to be a nun."

"Good," Flynn responded, his fist still twisting and wrenching her long hair. "If she's pure enough for God, she should meet with our pathetically low Comanchero standards."

Madelina heard a sudden burst of shrill laughter.

The McKillian woman was bubbling with sadistic delight.

Sutherland looked at her in blank astonishment. "Where do I find women like that?"

Flynn shrugged. "I guess you know which

rocks to look under." Then, glancing down at Madelina, he shouted, "Okay, Flaco, let's string the old buzzard up."

48

The looting of her home and the death of her brother had been bad.

But the next several minutes she would remember to her dying day.

She would never forget the rope man running the lasso through the snaffle ring of the mount's bridle, looping it through the cantle ring, around the cantle, then tying it off on the horn. She would remember how Flaco had attempted to put an Arbuckle's bag over her father's head, but Sutherland had stopped him.

"Forget it. Let him face his God open eyed."

She remembered Flaco saying to her father, "Do not squirm, amigo. Leave the noose knot *quién es*," right where it is, "and the neck will break easy. We did not grease the noose, so you must not twist or spin. The noose sticks, and it will tear your head off. So let us see what kind of *cojones* you have. Or what kind of *peón hideputa*," son of a whore, "you really are."

Her father had *muchos cojones*.

When the man at the hanging horse cracked his wristquirt across the roan's rump, the only sound out of the old man was his last Hail Mary, which ended abruptly after the words, "Blessed art thou..."

For one sickening second he was sliding off the roan's rump, dropping like a stone into bloody eternity, dropping, dropping, dropping, four short feet, that was all.

He jerked to a sudden, convulsive stop, one foot from life, no more.

The neck was crooked in the noose at a grotesque angle, and the body was drifting into a long, slow, agonizing spin. Agonizing for the quick, that is. It was clear that the dead, as Flaco had prophesied, felt nothing. Carlos hung there twisting slowly, slowly in the breeze, his neck sharply bent, his wrists lashed tightly behind his back, his hands turning blue.

He hung in abeyance, hoisted up to meet his God.

"Amigo," Flaco said to him softly, "the buzzards shall breakfast on your eyeballs."

Madelina looked away and said nothing. The blood on her cheek ran down her throat, through her ripped blouse, and over the heaving swell of her small, naked breasts. Slowly the jagged rip was beginning to clot.

"Damn," Lorenzo said quietly, "them noose knots sure get it done."

Flynn nodded. "Like God's own lightning bolts."

He released his grip on Madelina's hair.

Before she hit the ground, he was moving toward his horse.

Sutherland motioned him to stop.

"What is it?" Flynn asked.

"The bitch. I'm not sure she's told us everything."

For a moment Flynn looked as though he might object, then he shrugged. "Whatever you say."

"The old coot said she was to be a bride of Christ, correct?"

Flynn nodded.

"That is something she would not jeopardize for this outlaw friend of theirs."

"You mean...?"

"We told her father we would do it."

Flynn looked down at her. She was lying in a heap, covered with dirt, tears, and blood. He was silent.

"These men of yours have been eyeing the delectable Miss McKillian for weeks now. Let's see how manly they really are."

Flynn rubbed his nose pensively. "*All* of them?"

"Yes. If that doesn't shake the truth out of her, we can presume Slater's dead."

"And the search is off?"

"Yes, and your men get their bonus."

On the word *bonus* Flynn was already yelling, "Dismount!"

A split second later, amid a raucous din of creaking saddles and clinking bridle chains, the men were off their horses.

Quickly they crowded into line.

Madelina looked up. In the deepening twilight

gloom, she watched the twisted queue of battling men, confused at what they were fighting over.

At last, it came to her.

Hideously, piercingly, she began to scream.

49

Later that night, she came to. She could see nothing. The pain tore with steel claws at her head, down her back, then spread out through her thighs and down to her feet.

For a long while she lay there lost and alone, her moorings stripped. She had neither pole star nor handhold to find her way. She was blinded by nausea and vertigo.

She gradually became aware of the sick-sweet smell of coal oil. She rolled over in disgust and suddenly saw a wall of flames flaring through the inky smoke of the burning house.

She realized then why she hadn't seen it before.

Her face had been buried in the dirt.

Suddenly she wanted to plunge her face back into the ground.

She was seized by the sulfurous, stomach-turning stench of scorched flesh and burning hair, and it all came back to her. The bodies of her father and brother had been hauled into the house and stacked like pieces of cordwood, even as she was being raped. Gallons of coal oil had then been poured over them, the house, the ramada, even the chicken coop and the woodpile.

She remembered watching the remuda being rounded up and her father's pure-blooded ponies herded in with the Comancheros' cow-hocked crow-bait. She remembered chickens having their necks wrung, thrown into bags, and slung over pack horses. She remembered the corral posts being ripped out by the teams of horses.

She remembered watching these things while the men rutted on her.

She remembered them finishing. Two dozen Comancheros mounted up. Some of the men were rubbing their crotches and laughing.

The horses stood spraddle-legged and snorted nervously, their heads hung low.

She recalled the torch being tossed into their home; the place going up. Flames enshrouded the old roof, shooting fiery red-orange shafts through the roiling coal-black smoke, as the flesh inside crackled and sputtered.

Then Flynn was standing over her, his cocked .45 leveled between her eyes.

Sutherland's order was a harsh bark: "No!"

"What?" Flynn was confused.

"No point to it," Sutherland said with a twisted grimace. "She doesn't know anything."

There were two dozen harsh, rasping laughs with a shrill, piercing giggle ululating high above the din.

Judith McKillian's eerie tremolo.
The memory made Madelina shudder.

50

That was that.

Now she was lying on her side.

Her face was turned to the burning building.

After a while, the house exploded.

At first she was puzzled by the blast, but gradually she understood. The walls had disintegrated, and the blackened, smoldering ceiling beams had collapsed. That was all.

Afterward, there was nothing. Just Madelina, trapped beyond pain, tears, or even heartbreak, trapped in a world infinitely worse than the ghastliest horrors of her blackest nightmares.

Just limp, bleeding Madelina.

Lost and forgotten in some hideous back room of starkest hell.

And the flames roared above her, snarling at the dark.

PART XIV

51

Torn Slater sat on the edge of a soft feather tick. The two naked whores kneeling at his feet playfully fingered his scars. One was navigating the long red bayonet slash transversing his upper body from left groin to right shoulder. The other had her pinky in the puckered bullet hole just under his right clavicle.

The madam, Calamity Jane Cannary, sat on his knee, casually tracing the broad white welts of Yuma and Sonora prisons striping his back.

Slater worked assiduously on a quart of Old Crow.

All three women took turns fondling his cock.

Not that it did much good. The women had had him in the bed for thirteen hours straight and had engaged him in every position, perversion, and orgasm known to God and man. Each had had her turn at his various parts, he at theirs, they at one another's. The results had proved exhilarating, particularly for Calamity. Watching Slater in the throes of eros with two other women made her delirious with desire. When she watched Slater's amorous overtures to one or more of the other courtesans, his mouth vibrating voluptuously on their sundry orifices, Calamity felt that same forbidden flame blaze between her own thighs. She felt her heart pulse in her mouth and pound in her ears as if his furious heat were consuming her, too.

During that final hour, her lust, which had smoldered, smoked, and sparked all evening, caught fire and raged furiously out of control. It happened while the young redheaded whore named Rita massaged the head of Slater's cock with her tongue and lips. As Calamity watched, her clitoris mushroomed grotesquely. Clem's red-hot yearnings crackled through her like a flash-fire. Her need was overpowering. Her lust was ravenously aroused by the spectacle of young redheaded Rita working on Slater's member.

The sight of all that lust robbed Calamity of her reason.

For Calamity, this *Circus Maximus* had reached a crescendo pitch. Now it was all or nothing. Pushing Rita aside, she leaped onto Slater's massive member, and, grabbing him under the armpits, flipped herself onto her back, swinging him above her.

Instantly, they were fucking, both of them riding it hard, close to the wild beating heart of life. On and on they pounded, straight on through to the hell-hot core of the sun, fucking, fucking and fucking. Now Clem's irises were rolled back, and her eyes showed nothing but white. Her jaw was jacked open, and her head was rolling back and forth, back and forth. It was all

she could do to moan over and over, "Jesus
God...Jesus God...Jesus God..."

During her final orgasm, she came so hard
that she raked his ass repeatedly, her nails striping his buttocks bloody like cavalry spurs.

And when the final agony of passion ripped
through her, she thought she'd died and gone
to orgasm heaven.

52

But that was past.

Now Calamity sat on his lap, kissing him and
fondling his slack, useless member.

From time to time, Slater shared his bottle
with her, but mostly he stared out the window,
oblivious to them all.

Then Candy went to work. This distressed
Calamity. Candy was the lemon blonde with the
fiery temper, the one who favored lavishly shadowed eyes and shiny crimson lip paint with
gaudily matching nails. Candy wedged herself
between Slater's legs and around Calamity's feet.
Rising on her knees, she began giving Slater's
wasted member head.

In no time at all, Slater's privates were garishly

smeared with scarlet lip rouge, but his member was still limp as a toy balloon.

It was clear that his libido had it.

Finally, Calamity packed it in. She eased herself off his lap. Swaying lazily in the afterflush of her many orgasms, she swung her naked body over to the dresser mirror. She picked up a brush and began stroking her hair.

"Damn, you're old," Calamity said throatily. "Time was you could go all day *and* all night. Now, hell, fourteen or fifteen times, and you're impotent as that little fucker Paxton downstairs."

"Paxton ain't impotent," Rita said, leaping to J.P.'s defense.

Candy and Calamity stared at her.

"He's got what he calls pre-mat-cher-ee-jack-oo-lay-shon," Rita said.

Candy looked puzzled. "What's that?"

"It means he comes real fast."

"That ain't exactly great, is it?" Candy said.

"J.P. tells me it's real great," Rita explained. "Takes the pressure off him to perform."

Calamity glared at Rita, incredulous. "Sounds like the man I'm lookin' at right now."

Slater, still staring out the window, said, "Do *all* your rooms face backalleys?"

"Hell no," Rita answered for Clem. "Them curtained-off bolt holes downstairs, they don't have no windows at all."

Calamity now frowned at Slater. "That does it, cowboy. Time I found me something younger. Some fresh uncurried kid, a real range-run colt all sap and springtime. I'm purely wore out with you rundown, mossy-horned herd studs."

"Was he always this old?" Rita mocked, plunking her own naked derierre on Slater's knee.

"Hell, you should've seen him when he rode up on that poisoned wolf bait two months ago, all burned to hell, skin and bones, with a broken arm to boot. He weren't so proud then. Looked like a plucked pullet down with the croup and hopin' to die 'fore sunset. Now you look at him struttin stiff-legged 'round here, him and that pet lion calls himself a dog, you'd think they was Jeff Davis and Bobby Lee."

Slater inverted the bottle and lowered it three fingers.

Suddenly, Calamity's own dog, Princess, stuck her head in, pushing open the door. She gazed around curiously. Her eyes fixed on Slater's naked member, rudely smeared with crimson lip paint.

Her jaw gaped and her tail wagged wildly.

Slater met the dog's stare coolly. "Sorry, girl. You'd hate yourself in the morning."

"And I'd shoot you both," Calamity snarled.

She continued to examine herself in the mirror and brush her hair.

Slater glanced admiringly at Clem. She was perhaps a little old for the whore-lady business. Certainly not as youthful and fetching as, say, Rita or Candy, but he had to hand it to her. She was some woman.

What was it Clem had? Slater thought absently. One hell of a laugh. A really wonderful walk— back straight, arms swinging, long powerful strides. Pale skin, fine bones, pert breasts, a round firm bottom. And, of course, legs. Long, shapely, muscular legs.

After all, any lady who had hung on to Bill Hickok all those years had to have something.

Calamity turned. "Hell, Slater, you don't want us around for nothing 'ceptin' our snatches, do you, cowboy?"

"I like to think of them things as Keys to the Kingdom."

"Don't hand me none of that two-bit slickum. All you men're like that. All you want us women for is our pussies."

Slater shrugged. "Where is it written we gotta converse with you?"

Now all three glowered at Slater, but he ignored their womanly wrath. He turned his gaze instead to Calamity's mirrored reflection. Yes, he thought, it was true the face showed a few lines, but while she wasn't exactly a knockout anymore, she wasn't Bear Dog either.

Speaking of which . . .

Slater looked around the room curiously. "Say, any of you see that hound of mine?"

"Don't you try and change the subject," Calamity said, still brushing her hair.

"No, really. He ain't stuck his nose in here for six or eight hours. That ain't like him."

"Who the hell knows? Can't be out getting into no fights. Killed pretty near every dog in El Paso and Ciudad Juarez, to say nothin' of this here island. Outside of my Princess, leastways. Why? You concerned?"

Slater didn't answer. Once more he was staring at Clem's reflection in the mirror. He glanced absently at the hard flat stomach and the perky breasts. She brushed a fly away from her rear end, wiggling simultaneously, and his gaze fixed on the switching, satiny ass.

What an ass, he thought.

An ass to fly you to worlds where you've never been.

To worlds you've never even heard of.

"Who needs Bear Dog?" Rita whooped, being the first to notice it. "We got Torn Fucking Slater."

She and Candy instantly began piling on top of him, knocking the whiskey bottle out of his hand. It rolled across the floor and bounced off Calamity's heels.

She bent down, picked it up, and took a deep pull.

Then she gazed at the pileup on the bed.

The girls were kissing Slater all over while fondling his massive member.

Which was once again standing at attention.

Ramrod-straight as a Prussian drill sergeant.

"Hell with Bear Dog is goddamn right," Calamity yelled. "Move over, ladies, and make room for me."

She leaped across the bed onto all three.

53

"Hell with Bear Dog is goddamn right," Calamity had said.

And her statement fitted Bear's mood. Much as he liked his pack leader, Slater, he had to admit that the place he'd brought him to was almost as bad as the fucking pit.

He spent half his days and nights roaming the squalid streets of El Paso and Ciudad Juarez, looking for a dog to kill.

The pickings were slim. In Mexico the *peónes* ate the scrawny little fuckers, and in El Paso the street-bred dogs were wise enough to catch his scent and move on.

Mostly he just lumbered through the streets— as he was doing right now—growling softly to himself in a piss-poor frame of mind.

He hated to admit it, but in some ways the Comanchero camp had it all over these border towns. At least there was action. Here there were just a lot of bad smells: rotting sewage, filth and disease, the endless maelstrom of men's stinking emotions—hate and fear, lust and violence—all confused, contradictory.

He did not know how much longer he could take it.

For one thing, he did not have any clearly defined duties. In the Comanchero camp, his job had been to kill animals in the pit in exchange for Lorenzo's daily feeding. With Carlos's family his job had been to endure Madelina's obnoxious petting and to hunt marauding beasts. And while he would rather have been on the meat trail, in a land where there was food aplenty, pulling down bucks and flushing quail, at least pitfighting and tracking were *something*.

Here there was nothing.

Well, not exactly nothing. As Bear Dog lumbered toward the muddy riverbank for a cool evening swim, he thought that at least those endless games at the round green tables provided him with some diversion. His leader sat there several hours a night flicking colorful pasteboards around the table to five or six other gents. Bear Dog thought of these nightly rituals as potential action, because he smelled so much danger. The hot swirling scents of hate, fear, violence, and lust permeated everything when the pasteboards flashed.

During those moments he had to be on the alert. His leader was in constant danger. He could smell it.

And sure enough, there were manfights nightly.

But no dog fights.

For when the manfights occurred, his leader would rise from the table and take out his sidearm. He would then shoot some stranger dead or bend the big pistol over a stranger's hat. Once, when a cardplayer sitting next to his

leader had lunged at him with a knife, Slater
had disarmed the man, then gutted him throat
to balls with the man's own blade.

So, yes, while that constituted danger of a sort,
as far as action went it was unsatisfactory. For one
thing, despite the violent smells, his leader never
seemed to be in any trouble. Most times, before
Bear Dog could even work up a good growl, his
leader's gun was exploding, women were screaming, some new stranger lay bleeding and dying,
rudely spread-eagled across the floor, and there
was a surprised new face in hell.

It wasn't much fun, standing there stiff-legged,
fur bristling in waves, ears flat against his head,
lip curled in a feral snarl, fangs flashing and
frothing—and then have nothing to fight.

In fact, if Bear Dog was honest about it, the
most violent and dangerous smells always came
from his own leader.

In truth, Bear Dog thought wryly, if he wanted
action, he would, no doubt, have to jump *him*.

54

He was coming out of the Rio Grande, lumbering and grumping up the bank.

When he saw her.

Calamity's bitch, the one they called Princess, lying on the top of the rise, glaring at him coolly.

Waiting for him.

He stopped halfway and growled at her. Inside the brothel, his leader made him respect her, and he obeyed. Back there, Bear Dog viewed her as something belonging to his leader, mainly because they lived in the same house.

Hence, he was duty-bound to protect her.

But here, this far from home, well, he hadn't worked that one out yet.

There she was—a big shepherd, all browns and tans—glaring at him. Ordinarily, she kept her eyes lowered in his presence. Oh yes, she grinned and gallumphed around Calamity. She even gave paw to her mistress and fetched her slippers, which for some reason delighted that poor woman no end.

Yet here Princess was—sprawled on the top of the embankment in a half-circle, forepaws under her chest, tail under her nose, jaws flopped on hind paws, eyes staring at him unblinkingly.

Eye contact.

Meaning a direct challenge.

Bear Dog's upper lip curled in an ugly snarl. Princess meant business. She wasn't greeting him as she did her mistress, slippers in mouth, sneezing complacently—no, not at all. In fact, even as he stood there—stopped halfway up the bank, ambivalent as to whether he should fight her as a foe or protect her as one of his leader's possessions—she laid back her ears, stood stiff-legged and bristling, bared her teeth, and growled.

Suddenly Bear Dog froze, intense, alert. Something was wrong with the bitch. He could smell it. She had been following him, that was clear. She had picked up his trail, then tracked him on his nightly rounds through the streets, caught up with him, then followed him all the way to the river till she was sure they would be alone.

And headed him off.

And now—

Bear Dog continued to meet her gaze coolly, unamused, even as Princess's snarls soared with feral intensity. So that was the way she wanted to play, huh? Hard, tough, fast. Well, no matter. Bear Dog had handled a hundred bitch-wolves tougher than she, to say nothing of who knows how many dogs. Oh, he could tell she was formidable. There was no mistaking that. He would have to stay alert. But, on the whole, he was unconcerned.

Slowly he angled away from her on up the slope till he reached the top, giving her a wide berth. He sauntered off to the side, acting as if he might actually turn his tail to her and walk away.

Now her growls became almost rabid. She clearly could not believe that Bear Dog was giving her trail.

She shook her head. Her eyes darted back and forth. She turned her head down the other side of the river to see if—

Then Bear Dog struck. Attacking from the blind side, he grabbed her by the nape, shouldered her hard in the gut, and flung her muzzle-

over-tail down the long steep bank into the Rio
Grande.

She broke the river's surface, frightened, dripping wet.

Bear Dog glared at her contemptuously.

Quietly, patiently, he started back down the
steep embankment, one knowing step at a time.

55

Calamity Jane Cannary slowly descended the
long steep staircase of the Balcony Bar. She was
wearing a slinky red dress, elbow-high leather
gloves, and a pair of fashionable black boots
with elegant two-inch heels. Her only jewelry
was a simple silver brooch inlaid with turquoise.
She wore it at her throat, pinned to a black
ribbon that was tied off snugly behind the
nape.

Calamity looked over the crowded bar.

The main room was doing a land-office business. She saw big games everywhere—draw, stud,
blackjack, red dog, faro, keno, craps, and rou-
lette at dozens of layouts. The room rang with
cries: "Ante's a buck," "Two on the lady," "Deal-
er calls," and "Three little gents." The air crackled with ratcheting whir of the big wheels, the

rattle of the bones, and the constant flick of pasteboards across the baize. A score of hard-nosed trail hounds bellied up to the long bar, their boot heels hooked over the brass footrail. Two to three gents were standing beside their soiled doves in front of each of the curtained-off bolt holes, awaiting their chance at the painted ladies. Eight massive brass chandeliers, sur-mounted by conical top shades of white dam-ask, spread great circles of light around the room, most of it focused on the gaming tables. The light from the chandeliers' guttering can-dles jumped and flickered. The rest of the room was illuminated by coal-oil lamps bracketed against the walls.

The draped-off bolt holes were intentionally kept dark.

A big cowboy, his arm around the luscious, tawny-haired Lucy, lumbered up the steps. He tipped his ten-gallon Stetson to Calamity and mumbled, "Howdy, ma'am," as he hustled the girl up toward one of the more expensive rooms.

Lucy gazed at him demurely, full of bogus charm and false smiles.

In a far corner the piano man, dressed in a white boiled shirt, a red bow tie, and matching elbow garters, banged out "Red River Valley" on the ancient, rickety upright. A half-dozen schoon-ers of beer were lined up atop the piano, cadged off the high rollers during his break.

A cigarillo dangled from his lips as he boomed out the lyrics.

Calamity studied the room carefully. There, at a small, dimly lit corner table, sat Slater and

J.P. Paxton, whom they generally called the Professor.

She headed down the steps toward her seat.

56

Paxton wore a slate-gray claw-hammer coat, a matching bowler, and a floral-patterned brocade vest. His shirt was white raw silk, and his wire-rimmed spectacles were perfectly round.

The lenses were as thick as the bottoms of whiskey glasses.

He was apple-cheeked and inveterately cheerful. He smiled pleasantly at Calamity's approach.

Slater, on the other hand, looked funereally grim in his black frock coat, matching black vest, and black Stetson. His short-cropped black beard and flat black eyes, and the big black hound lying alongside him, muzzle resting on crossed paws, did nothing to brighten his grave appearance.

Calamity pulled out a straight-backed chair and sat down.

"See you found that damn dog," she said, helping herself to a shot from the bottle of Old Crow.

"Yeah. He come in here an hour or so ago, all tore up but struttin' and stiff-legged."

"Speakin' of dogs, you ain't seen anything of Princess?" Clem asked. "She missed her evenin' feed, which, to put it mildly, is uncharacteristic."

"Yeah, that damn cur could eat the ass out of a rag doll," Slater agreed. "But she's in the back room, sawin' wood."

"She's asleep?" Clem asked incredulously.

"Like she was dead. Like she could sleep through Antietam."

Calamity shook her head, astonished.

A gent in a brown broadcloth shirt and a tan plainsman's hat strolled up to them. He was half in the bag. "Nice dog," he said, reaching down to pet him.

"Wouldn't do that, mister," Slater said.

"Ain't afraid of no damn dog."

"Don't bullyrag the Bear. He'll take your hand off at the wrist."

"Say he's mean?"

"Mean enough to kill a rock. Now cut and drift."

The man looked at Slater, angered. "Hey, I hope there ain't no hard feelings, mister. I'd purely regret there was hard feelings."

"That's all I got."

Calamity concurred. "Only thing tender 'bout this gent's his temper. Now mosey."

The man stared at Slater a long second, as if trying to place him or even attempting to make something of it. He thought better. He gave them an insincere smile.

"Ah, hell, maybe I ought to just take one of these soiled doves upstairs."

Calamity nodded and poured herself another slug of Old Crow. She waved him away, indifferent. "See you on campus."

The Professor gave Slater a searching look. "I hope you're not as violent as they say?"

"Comes as readily to him as drawing breath," said Calamity.

Slater turned to Clem, his eyes filled with mockery. "You suggestin' I be a wrongdoer?"

"I'd say you're a little less'n the sum of your failings."

"You suggestin' I didn't make it upstairs?"

"You just watch that, boy. Too much pleasure destroys."

"You mean that didn't soap your saddle up there?"

Calamity smiled sweetly. "It wound my watch."

Paxton cleared his throat, obviously embarrassed by the tone of the conversation. "Miss Calamity, I hate to be critical of your life's work, but this is truly a wretched place. Whatever brought you here?"

Calamity shrugged. "I was searchin' for my identity."

"Any luck?" Slater asked.

"All of it bad. I think I found it."

"Miss Calamity," the Professor said, "this is hardly a fitting environment for a woman of your dignity and bearing. Are you sure you can't find something better to do with your life?"

"All I want is to start sellin' my pussy less

often for more pesos." She rubbed her crotch and belted down another shot.

"Maybe I'm the one who's out of place here," the Professor said glumly.

"I'll say," Slater agreed. "'Bout as out of place as a nigger saint in Natchez."

"What *are* you doin' down here anyway?" Calamity asked. "I ain't seen you since Deadwood."

The Professor cleared his voice. "Well, I've been having a few problems lately. Can't seem to come up with any new material for my poems and songs."

"You came up with enough to half-ruin my career, what with that 'Ballad of Outlaw Torn Slater' shit you been writin'," Slater grumbled.

"Yes, but quite frankly that well has run dry. I thought perhaps if I left New York, came west again, found you two, I might also find myself. Who I am, what I am. I might give my work some new, hard-won authenticity. But so far all I've found is Miss Calamity destroying herself in his miserable place. Mr. Slater, doesn't this horrid establishment distress you?"

Slater glanced around at the gaudily painted whores and their Johns. "The joint always looked to me like Shiloh with lipstick."

Paxton disagreed. "Miss Calamity shouldn't be here. Look at her. Does she look like some common harlot to you?"

Slater looked her up and down noncommittally. "Maybe not. But she sure don't look like no lady, neither."

"You're not going to tell me Miss Calamity is one of these sordid sluts?" Paxton said.

Slater started laughing. "Hell, Clem here'll fuck anything, anyplace, anytime. She'll fuck on cactus. On a goddamn anthill."

Paxton, clearly agitated, attempted to throw back a shot of whiskey. However, he gagged on it, and it drizzled down his chin and onto his floral-patterned brocade vest.

"Careful, Professor," Calamity said, "some of it's getting in your mouth."

"My God," he groaned, "this is truly execrable stuff."

"I be your witness there," Slater agreed and knocked back four fingers.

Seeing the piano man stand to take a break, Paxton said, "I think I'll sit a spell at the piano. Perhaps music shall soothe my savage breast."

After he got up, Clem stared at Slater. "Anything special *you* ever wanted out of life?"

"Sure. High cards, solid colors."

"That all?"

He shrugged. "Pussy, tequila, fists full of pesos."

Calamity groaned.

The opening piano refrain of Paxton's song drifted through the bar, a slow lilting ballad, and Calamity winced.

"What's that song?" Slater asked.

Clem stared at the bottle and poured herself another drink. "It's called 'Calamity.' It's 'bout me and Hickok."

The song began:

> Bill's gone away,
> Calamity.
> Your Wild Bill you'll see no more.

HELL HOUND

You feel the flash and hear the roar
And see his brains upon the floor.
He's gone away forevermore.
He's gone,
Calamity.

Slater stared at her dumbstruck.

The man who shot him from behind
Was Sudden Jack McCall.
Who had the guts to face the swine
Who murdered Wild Bill?
The decent folk? They weren't that kind.
That hand they could not fill.
You want justice, Calamity Jane?
McCall you'll have to kill.

When he leaves, you don't think twice.
You go after Jack McCall.
You find him drinkin'n shootin' dice
Inside a gamblin' hall.
You nail the bastard by surprise,
You nail him by his balls.
Your big-bore Sharps against his guns
Is a bet he will not call.

But why should Sudden Jack McCall
Want to face you down?
The men who bought that evil killin',
Hell, they owned the town.
They bought the judge and paid the jury.
By nightfall Jack was gone.
And you just stood there unbelievin'
With Hickok underground.

Bill's gone away,
Calamity,
Your Wild Bill you'll see no more.
You feel the flash and hear the roar
And see his brains upon the floor.
He's gone away,
Calamity.
He's gone forevermore.

"That shit popular?" Slater asked, astonished.
"'Bout as popular as bourbon, poker, and pussy."
"I'll be damned."
"Wait. It gets worse."

McCall is in the Badlands.
He thinks you'll lose his trail.
You'll lose his trail when he's dead
Or rottin' in some jail.
You'll track his sad ass straight to hell
And hear his damned soul wail.
You're on his ass while you got breath,
His hide you swore to nail.

You catch him in the Badlands.
This time they ain't so kind.
That very day he's damned to hang,
The noose you're there to twine.
With thirteen turns you cinch his knot.
You're pleased to hear him whine.
The man who killed the man you love,
You're there to watch him die.

Slater smiled gently. "Don't feel bad. You should hear what he writes about me. In one of the songs, he claims all my friends are dead."

"Ain't they?"

Slater furrowed his brow in thought. "Cole Younger's in prison."

"Yeah? Well, in this one, he claims *I'm* dead."

"What?"

"He even writes my fuckin' epitaph. Here. Catch to the rest of it."

> In the end you give up the ghost
> Your day is finally done.
> They bury you with the one you lost.
> Hickok, home she's come.
> For more than dreams your life he cost.
> For all your hopes lie torn.
> More than love, your soul he cost,
> For all your life you've mourned.
>
> Many strive for cold cruel gold,
> And others oceans rove.
> Some rob trains with hearts so bold;
> A few seek God above.
> Fate's false fleet dice all men have rolled.
> For art, some mortals strove.
> A whore's sweet flesh some ache to hold.
> Calamity, you died for love.

The standing ovation was thunderous. Paxton stood, took several bows, and blew kisses to the whores. Meanwhile, Slater leaned over to Clem.

"That stuff ain't true 'bout you mournin' for Hickok all these years, is it?"

"Maybe. Yeah, I think of him a lot. But there's

others around. There's them could fill his boots. If they wanted to."

"Hickok's? No way." Slater averted his eyes. "He was so high up there he scraped his boots on the stars."

Calamity shrugged. "You thought a lot of him, didn't you?"

"He was one of a kind."

"Not really. You're a lot like him. He always said so."

"We worked different sides of the street. He even lawed."

"Not when he busted you out of Yuma."

Slater smiled. "That's a lock."

"He thought a lot of you, too. So do I." She said the last words quickly, then was sorry, embarrassed at the sentiment.

Slater said nothing. After a long moment, he poured himself another drink and slugged it down. The applause was at last dying down. Paxton, shrugging off the cries of "Encore! Encore! Encore!" made his way back to their table.

57

Slater was just tapping the bottle for another shot when Rita came to the table and sat down.

She was decked out in a tight green dress swagged at the hip, and her long red hair was piled high on her head.

"Nice song, Professor," Rita said.

"How's business?" Paxton asked.

"Gets any busier I'll need a steel snatch."

The Professor winced.

Clem glanced around the crowded room. "'Pears that way. Rate it's goin', I could use some more girls."

Rita helped herself to the bottle. "There's one 'round back I think's applyin'. Come up askin' for Torn Slater." Rita gave Slater a strange look. "I know how sensitive you are 'bout your identity and all, so I just sent her on the way."

Slater rubbed his nose. "Maybe she was just one of my many admirers. Was she good-lookin'?"

"Maybe. Couldn't tell, she was so damn tore up."

"Don't sound promising."

"She ain't," Rita said. "Come here wadin' through the river with nothin' 'cept the few filthy clothes on her half-naked back. Looked like a side of raw meat drug through dry dirt, like somethin' ain't et in three days."

"Bring her back and get her somethin' to eat," Calamity said.

"Aw, hell," said Rita, "you go feedin' every starvin' Mex girl comes 'round here, this place'll be a soup kitchen 'steada a whorehouse."

"Is she truly destitute?" the Professor asked.

"She ain't got nothin' to eat, spend, or trade."

"Oh, she's got somethin' she can trade," Slater offered dryly.

"I ain't so sure," said Rita.

"Thought you described her as a woman," Slater said.

"Yeah, but life done played a tune on her head. Or I should say on her face. Someone worked it over with what looks like a stiletto. Four or five long red scars zigzaggin' down her cheek."

"Sounds like somethin' a 'Pache would do," said Slater.

"Or a dog-mean pimp," Rita suggested.

"Get her somethin' to eat," Calamity repeated.

Rita's expression was quizzical. "Still can't get over her sayin' she knows you. She just don't look like your type."

"They're all his type. Eight to eighty. Blind, crippled, or crazy. Just as long as they be female and breathin'," Clem said.

"Well, she ain't no white woman, that's for sure. Looks tough as a turkey vulture too, real down on her hustler's luck. 'Cept that she keeps sayin' something 'bout wantin' to be a nun but can't no more. Says she ain't pure enough. Said you'd know what she meant. Ain't that a hoot. Slater here gettin' it on with a bride of Christ."

"She didn't leave no name, did she?" Slater's voice was strangely hoarse.

"Funny you ask. I said to her, 'Look, sister, you a nun, I be Mary Magdeline. And she said, 'I am Madelina. Tell Señor Slater, I am Madelina.' At which point I knew she was crazy and told her to fuck off."

"Get her somethin' to eat," Calamity started to say again.

But suddenly Slater was up and heading for the back room at a run.

58

Slater, with Calamity close behind, found Madelina still waiting at the back door. He quickly got her into the kitchen, and by then Calamity was on the case. Clem got her a lot more than something to eat.

She gave Madelina a long hot scrub in the big claw-footed tub upstairs, her best flannel dressing gown, and a chance to rest.

When Madelina was ready to come back down, they met in the kitchen.

59

They sat in the kitchen at the big round oak table—Clem, Slater, Paxton, Rita, and Madelina.

Calamity had gotten out more chicken, frijoles, tortillas, and a pitcher of milk.

The girl told her story tersely. When she finished, she stared across the table at them. Her gaze was calm, empty eyed, unafraid.

"What was the trip here like?" Calamity asked.

"Muy malo"—very bad—she said. "I was no longer welcome in the convent because I was impure." She could see anger contort Calamity's face, and said quickly, "It was no great matter. I had lost interest in bearing witness for Christ and doing His work."

"Why was that?" the Professor asked.

"I had to cross much of Mejico penniless and afoot to get to the convent, and later to get here. The journey was a rude awakening. Everywhere I went I found our people hungry, diseased, poor, frightened, broken in spirit, and in chains. I had been taught by the priests that peacemakers were divinely blessed, but in the world I witnessed, those teachings made no sense. Violence was universal; peace, rare."

"Peace ain't rare," Slater said quietly. "It don't exist."

Madelina turned to him. "That was the other thing that bothered me. What you told us at the ranchero. You said that loving one's enemies might succeed in a lunatic asylum but not in Chihuahua. You said that some men might be converted to Christ's Word, but not the ones after you. You said only a flogging post, a rack, or a gallows could win their hearts and minds. At the time I thought you the worst man who ever lived, no better than the ones on your backtrail. But I met those men, and I learned what they were like. And I know now the sort of man you are."

"What kind is that?" Calamity asked.

"Their enemy. A man whom they hate and fear so much that they trapped, tortured, and tried to kill. Señor, I have also studied that wanted poster on you, and have asked myself what kind of man would have a warrant on him like that."

"Genghis Khan? Attila the Hun?" Calamity speculated.

"No, what I saw was something different. I saw in that poster a man's life. I saw his strengths and abilities. I saw a man who could do what was necessary, who could kill if he had to."

"Aw, hell," Rita said, "Torn can do lots of things real good besides killin'. Can't he, Clem?"

"Like what?" Calamity asked.

Rita shrugged. "Oh, you know."

"Yeah? Besides fuckin' women, dealin' seconds, and drinkin' whiskey—what?"

"He robs banks and trains real good," Rita said admiringly.

Slater leaned across the table toward Madelina. "Ignore them. What is it you want?"

Madelina stared back at Slater, her eyes cold. "These people who did this to me and to my family, I no longer believe they should find their justice in the hereafter, nor do I believe that peacemakers are divinely blessed. What I want is for these people to suffer, even as they made my family suffer. As they made me suffer."

"How do you propose this, honey?" Calamity asked. "You got a whole gang of Comancheros, plus an international tycoon, after you. Hell, from what I hear, old Porfirio Diaz might even deal himself in. You even know how to find them?"

"I'll find them," Madelina said simply.

Slater shook his head. "You wouldn't know which rocks to look under."

"Perhaps Calamity could help," Rita suggested.

"Sure, if pussy was bullets, she could kill France. But it ain't. And she won't be much help against that camp of Comancheros."

"What do you suggest?" Madelina asked.

"Well, if you want me to bring back the rack, the wheel, and the iron maiden, and make them suffer as they made you suffer, I can't. Hell, the *federales* and the U.S. Army's been after them boys for years, and I ain't no one-man Seventh Cavalry. But, yeah, if you want me to hurt them, to make them feel some of what you feel, sure, I can do that."

"You're gonna take on two dozen professional killers holed up in a fortified mountain camp?" Calamity was incredulous.

"Seems like I don't have much choice."

"And that don't shake you none?" Calamity asked.

"Like the wind in the trees."

"And just how are you gonna commit this one-man massacre?" Rita asked.

"I ain't got to that part yet. S'pose it'll take some schemin'. But I 'spect there's a way."

"What are we into now? Assassination? Torture? Terrorism?"

"The word Señor Sutherland used to describe his actions was *heroism*."

J.P. Paxton looked at Slater dubiously. "My friend, what you're suggesting is utterly illegal."

Everyone laughed except Paxton and Madelina.

"What is so funny?" Madelina asked. "What I want *is* illegal, is it not?"

Even Clem had to snort. "Nothin' Slater's associated with's ever been legal."

"Yes, but I see nothing funny."

"It'll come to you," said Calamity.

Madelina still looked confused.

"Don't worry, honey," said Rita. "What you require right now is someone totally without principles, and I suspect you've come to the right place."

Madelina crossed herself quickly and muttered a prayer.

Paxton looked the girl straight in the eye. "Señorita, I believe you should reconsider your request. You are not looking for this man's help. You are looking for Charon, the ferryman to hell."

Calamity shook her head. "This will not have a happy ending."

"Do not fear, Miss Calamity," Madelina said. "I shall look after Señor Slater."

Now it was Slater's turn to look surprised.

"You wanna work my side of the street?" he asked. "Sorry, kid. Hell, we ain't even in the same neighborhood."

"I must."

Slater shook his head. "You'd be like a fish floppin' on the riverbank. You'd be out of your element."

"Pardon me for being so eternally dumb,"

Paxton asked, "but isn't this just a very complicated way of committing suicide?"

"You tell him, Professor," Calamity said.

"These Comancheros. What did you say they do for a living?"

"Rape, murder, torture, dismemberment," Slater said.

"And you think to take them on all alone?"

"I shall be there too," Madelina repeated.

Slater looked at her irritably. .

"And I say you shall not make it," the Professor said.

"And I say," Slater argued, "we got a tremendous advantage."

The whole table stared at him.

"What is that?" Rita finally asked.

"They think I'm dead."

"I don't believe this is happening," Calamity said gloomily.

"Clem, buck up," said Slater, grinning. "The winds of war are blowin'."

60

It was early morning, and Rita was ready to go to bed. The rest of the group had turned in hours ago. She stopped by the kitchen for a cup of Arbuckle's and found Madelina still there. She was wearing Calamity's long flannel dressing gown. Rita sat beside her.

Madelina looked pleased. "I like the people here *muy bueno*. I'm so glad Señor Slater got ahold of Miss Calamity."

"Oh, he done that all right. He does it all the time."

Madelina gave Rita a curious stare.

"I'm also glad he accepted. I do not know how I could have gone on otherwise."

"What would you have done if he'd said no?"

"Yelled, argued, fought, I do not know."

Candy, the fiery blonde, walked into the kitchen. She was still decked out in her working clothes, a black slinky evening gown of sheerest satin, swagged at the hip.

"You'd've fought Torn Slater?" Candy asked.

"Or reasoned with him," Madelina said with conviction.

"You might have appealed to his better instincts," Rita suggested mockingly.

"Oh," Candy said with elaborate sarcasm, "you mean she might've offered him money?"

Madelina ignored the barb. "Tell me, what is Señor Slater really like?"

There was no more joking.

"Little girl, you best not find out," Candy said.

"But do we not join battle in common cause? Do we not share the same enemies?"

"I ain't talkin' Comancheros. I'm talkin' *you. You* best watch out for that man."

Madelina shook her head emphatically. "I do not think he will hurt me."

Candy gave Madelina a long, appraising look. "Sure, he'll hurt you. He'll hurt you bad. Just like he's hurt a hundred like you before, Clem included."

"I do not believe that. Look what he is doing. Risking his life against such evil men."

"Sure," Rita said, sipping her coffee, "I know. Now you think he's brave, strong, and true. And maybe he is, in his own way."

"So?"

"So in the end, when the problem's done and your trouble's over, he'll leave you. That's all. You won't know when or where or why. He'll just be gone, that's all. And you'll be alone."

"With your heart broken and your throat smokin'," Candy said.

"I do not understand such things," Madelina said.

"Just don't get to likin' him too much, that's all," Candy said.

"And keep out of his bedroll," Rita added. "'Cause one day he'll slip the bit. And if you get a feelin' for him, the hurt'll go hard."

"How do you know these things?" Madelina asked.

"You been with as many cold-blooded bastards as us, you get to know them, that's all. From childhood to senility, men like them's all the same. They're born to bring you down."

Madelina shrugged off the words. "It does not matter. Even if I cared, what man would want somebody like me? My face scarred, my body violated by so many men. I shall live out the balance of my life as chaste as if I were, in truth, a nun."

"You just stay that way awhile. 'Cause one day he'll jump the fence. And if you care for him, the hurt'll be harder."

61

Upstairs, Calamity and Slater lay in bed. They'd just made love, and in the afterflush she smoked a cigarillo. Slater sipped his whiskey.

"You serious 'bout takin' on them Comancheros?" Clem asked, breaking the silence, "or is that just some kind of shuck?"

"I'm gonna give it a try."

"I ain't gonna stand for it, you know."

"It's like I ain't got no other choice."

"You ain't even got a plan."

"I'll work out somethin'. I got ideas."

"Like hell you do."

"Look, Clem, if you're worried 'bout me and her out there on the llano, I don't give a rat's ass 'bout no—"

"Goddamn you to hell, I don't care 'bout your fuckin' women. I ain't sayin' this 'cause I'm jealous. Hell, I bring women to you. I even go to bed with them for you. No one woman can hold you, and I don't 'spect I will either. I always knew that. But, damm it, I figured you'd be with me for a while."

"I am with you." He tried to put his arm around her, but she threw it off.

"That ain't the fuckin' answer, Torn. The plain truth is I sprung you from Yuma Prison. I fought them heathen 'Paches for you. I went after them James-Younger boys with you after they turned on you in Tucson. And when you rode in here bleedin', broken, and sun-scorched half to death, I took you in and got you on your feet."

"Clem, I—"

"But no more. You hear me? No more. You ride out on me this time, on some insane—what was it the Professor called it?—'complicated way of committin' suicide', I'm tellin' you, that tears it."

"After what them boys done to her and her own, it's like *I* did it. Them people took me in, cared for me, and now they're dead and she's maimed. Clem, there's some things you don't leave undone. I figured you'd understand."

Clem smoked her cigarillo and nodded slowly. "Oh, I understand all right. I understand your goddamn code. Code says a man fucks with you like a man, you gonna kill him like a man. And since you rob banks and trains for a livin', men fuck with you all the time. So you spend half your life in jail, on the run, or trackin' some poor asshole down 'cause he got in your way, got on your case, or just didn't want you takin' his money."

"It ain't like that."

"I say it is. And I say no more. It ends here."

"It don't end while they're 'bove ground."

"We could've had a life together. You know that?" Now Calamity was crying. "I got some money saved.

"Me, Calamity Jane. Can you imagine it? I ain't never saved a nickel in my life, but I been puttin' it away. I was puttin' it away for you. For us."

"I'll be back."

"No, you won't. You ride out of here, I don't want you ridin' back."

"I just can't let it be."

"Yeah, I know, it's your fuckin' code. Well, let me ask you this: What's that damn code ever done for you?"

He could not answer. He'd lived by these rules all his life. And they'd all but destroyed him.

Yet the code contained a power he could not deny.

He could not walk away from it.

Calamity continued, "The only other man I ever loved was Hickok, and he died on me. You're fixin' to do the same."

"I ain't cashed my stack yet."

"You might as well. You're always ridin' out on thems that love you. Ain't that the same thing?"

For a long time he was silent.

"What do you want?" he asked.

"I don't know. The law wants you dead. Them

Comancheros want you dead. The Mex government wants you dead. The United fuckin' States of America wants you dead. The entire free-market private-enterprise system of the world wants you dead. I guess I don't. Do you understand that? I want you alive. Meanin' I don't want you ridin' out with that girl."

"Anything else, Clem. Name it, it's yours. But not this."

"Okay. One thing. I want you to fuck me. Right now. I want you to fuck me like the world was ending at sunup. I want something I can remember you by. Something for all the times when you're on the run or doin' time or below the ground or just plain gone. Then I want you to leave and never come back. But in the meantime I want something to remember you by. I want one that'll last."

PART XV

62

Bear Dog trotted alongside the two horses and the pack mule with his tireless wolf's lope.

And was happy.

After all those endless months in those miserable border towns of El Paso and Ciudad Juarez and that wretched little sandspit of Esmeraldo, he was free.

He was back on the trail.

He even liked the way his leader and his mistress looked. Peak-crowned straw sombreros with the three-foot brims, white shirts of coarse-woven maguey, and *chaparreras*, or leggings, of good tough rawhide. They had big mounts, eight hundred pounds apiece. His leader's horse was a hammerheaded, barrel-bellied dun, the girl's a deep-chested gray. They were powerful animals with heavily muscled fore- and hindquarters, obviously picked for a long trek through the desert llano.

For extra mounts they'd picked two tough little range-raised mustangs, trail-wise and able to live off the land.

He even liked the pack mule, which was rare

for Bear Dog. His leader had picked out a mountain and desert-wise jack. This pack animal had the most calm, levelheaded disposition Bear Dog had ever known in a mule. Except for the single violent episode when he had reared away from a strike-coiled diamondback, Bear Dog had never seen him do more than wall his eyes, shrug his long rabbitlike ears, and snort noncommittally.

It was obvious that extreme care had gone into the selection of these animals.

It was obvious, too, that they had been chosen for a long, rough, arduous journey.

Just the sort of junket Bear Dog needed to whip himself back into shape.

63

They rode.

They rode through a flat thirsty desert with nothing in sight save the dim, distant specter of the *cordillera* floating on the horizon like an armada at sea in the shimmering heat haze. This was virgin llano, with no wheel ruts to follow, no voice heard save the dry moan of the wind, the unending drone of the locusts, the buzz of the flies. This was a land that witnessed no vision save the blinding, white-hot glare of the sun at zenith, and felt no caress save its pounding, pulsing heat, palpable as a hammer blow to the neck.

Five hundred miles of dead-still, dead-hot desert.

Five hundred miles of trackless, infernal waste.

Five hundred miles to that hell pit the Comancheros called home.

Five hundred miles.

They rode.

64

Each morning was the same.

Bannock bread, breakfast Arbuckle's boiled in an old feed measure, whatever measly jackrabbits or ground squirrels Bear Dog could run down or Slater could shoot. The big mounts and their extra ponies had originally been range bred and forage raised, and they were again on a regimen of prickly-pear pulp, mesquite beans, and bark from an occasional tree.

Each night was equally repetitive. They sat around the flickering glare of a canyon fire, watching the grotesque shadow figures dance on the far walls, wondering silently how long the water would hold out. Madelina observed that the llano was drier than she'd ever seen it, drier than a cinderblock. Slater, giving her that wry, infectious grin—one designed to melt cap ice off the rimrock or the hinges off an honest woman's hope chest—promised not to say it was "drier'n a nun's cunt."

And Madelina sat there not knowing what to think, let alone how to respond.

So she'd just stare into the fire, nodding, listening to the nighttime drone of the locusts, to the solitary barking coyote whose squalling sounded like a whole pack of hounds but who was too cunning for even Bear Dog to track down. She sat there listening to the whooshing swoop of the bug-feeding nighthawks and the rest of the desert's timeless cacophony.

And she wondered what they would find at the end of the line.

65

They rode.

They reached the *cordillero* in six weeks. Now they were heading up an endless maze of winding arroyos that would eventually lead them to the summit. These wash trails were rimmed by

thirty-foot gorge walls of red clay and sandstone, trails where, when the wind blew, the
sand and grit caked up in the corners of their
eyes, clogged their noses, and gummed up between their teeth. Then the wet bandannas came
out and were pulled over nose and mouth.

But still the blowing sand got through.

These were trails you picked your way through
carefully. Mesquite thorns, prickly pear, cat claw,
and the long, sharp bayonet spears of the yucca
challenged their passage at every turn. Canvas
chest aprons were taken out for the stock, and
the pack mule, which was the most surefooted
of the animals, led the way. Up the mountain
passes they rode, the heat rising around them
like steam, their eyes, noses, and mouths filled
with grit, their *chaparreras,* or chaps, slashed to
ribbons by the impenetrable jungle of throns.

Up the *cordillera.*

They rode.

66

Halfway up they made an early camp. They
staked out the stock in a cutbank near some
good forage and rubbed them down, working
grease into the saddle galls. After watering them,

they headed for another gorge in which they could make their own camp. Slater set the fire and boiled their evening Arbuckle's while Madelina fried up jackrabbit and pan bread. When Slater was finished smashing and grinding the beans between flat rocks, he threw them into the boiling water along with the dinner's hardtack.

Which needed considerable soaking and softening.

Madelina knew something was up. She knew it when he made the early camp and moved their sleeping quarters away from the horse picket. She finally got around to asking the question.

"How far are we from the Comanchero camp?"

"We're gettin' close enough to be cautious."

"Amigo, you still have not told me your plan."

"I know."

"Is it dangerous?"

Slater started laughing. "It ain't dangerous. It's insane."

"Tell me, *compadre,* are all your ventures so desperate?"

"That ain't the half of it."

"Does it not frighten you?"

"Ah, hell, it's what I been doin' twenty-five years now."

"Does that not bother you?"

Slater rubbed his nose and stared pensively into the fire. "I don't know. Don't seem like I changed much over them years. A few more scars. A little more restless."

"You're older, though."

"Yeah, I be older."

"And your friends and the places you've been, have they not changed?"

"My friends, as the Professor points out, are dead. Places? Yeah, they've changed. Shiloh's just a church again. Lawrence, Kansas, got some menfolk now. Hear some Temperance League ladies chopped up all the bars in Dodge."

"Are you afraid?"

"It don't work that way."

"What do you mean?"

"I'm more concerned with how we're gonna get this done. Them Comancheros are pretty tough. We don't pull this off right, it'll be hell with a busted cinch.

"Tell me about these men."

Slater scratched his head. "Them Comancheros? It's like they think they're half-dead already. They'd just as soon someone push it. They don't care if they end up the rest of the way."

"But you are tough too, no?"

Slater had to laugh at that one. "You should've seen me time-when."

"I am pleased with you now."

"So you're the one."

"It is not funny. To you everything is funny. You always make jokes. Well, you are my *compadre* and I do not make jokes. I say this from my heart. I am glad you do this thing for me. Even if we fail we will have tried. For this I am glad."

Slater nodded.

She was silent a long moment. "Señor, I know I have no right, but may I ask you one more favor?"

Slater shrugged. "Sure."

"I have this twin sister. She is not like me. She swerved from the sacred life and followed Satan's path. She met a boy who took her to Chihuahua. This boy is very bad. He made her a sinful woman. She now works in an evil place there and sees men. This man lives off her money."

He was tempted to say, "Oh, they're like me and Clem," but kept still.

"Well, this man is *muy malo* and very dangerous. I did not think until I met you that anybody was strong enough to take her away from this wicked life. But you could. I know you could. You could make her see her mistake and rescue her from Chihuahua."

"It ain't exactly my line of work."

"You mean you can't?"

"I got to be honest with you. Meaning, I just don't see how. I kinda draw the line at reformin' whores."

They were both silent a long time.

"Well," Slater said finally, "we got a long hard day tomorrow, so I suggest you turn in. When you find out what I got planned, you're gonna need all your strength."

"Still I say it. I am *muy* glad you are here."

He smiled gently. "Don't be too quick. When you see what I got planned, you may not be so thrilled. In fact, you may be downright discouraged."

"It does not matter. We are doing this thing. And now, this day, this moment, I am pleased."

67

Early that morning, Slater felt a tug at his arm.
Even before she touched him, his hand was out
from under his blanket, the big Colt in his fist.

"My friend," Madelina said, "I fear the day
shall go hard."

"I warned you."

"So at some point will you not give up? Will
you not quit?"

"You're the one who's weakenin'."

Madelina shook her head once. Decisively.

"No. Never. And, furthermore, I say that you
are my *hombre*. I say this to you even after our
friends in El Paso warned me not to say it. I say
it even though I have been used and defiled by
Comancheros. Even though my face is disfigured
and the convent declares me impure. I say this
knowing that no man will ever want me. Still I
say you are my *hombre*. Time-when. For-all-
tomorrows. I am not much of a *mujer,* I realize
that. After what those men did to me, I can
never enjoy what is shared between men and
women. Still, I will be faithful to you and cook
for you and, if you so desire, sleep with you."

"But you wouldn't enjoy it none?"

"Never. *Nada*."

Slater gently touched the scars along her cheek. Slowly he guided her hands under his shirt and allowed her to trace the long red bayonet scar transversing his chest, the puckered bullet hole just under his clavicle, and the broad white whip slashes of Yuma and Sonora prisons striping his back.

"Never?" he asked softly.

"Never."

68

Later that night, as his tongue gently worked its way around the little button that had become so inflamed with delight, she bit her knuckle and rasped, "Oh!...Oh!...Oh!..."

Later she buried her face in his chest and said, sobbing, "I did not think it possible. I never dreamed. You have mended the broken pieces and made me whole. I am indeed your *mujer,* and you are my *hombre*. My only *hombre,* now and forever. My *muy hombre*."

69

Eventually she fell asleep.

Slater lay on his back and stared blankly into the desert night sky awash with a dazzlingly bright moon and a vast carpet of unwinking stars.

What have you done? he said silently to himself. What the hell have you done?

PART XVI

70

The next morning, after working their way up the twisting gorge for several hours, Slater entered a narrow canyon. The pass wound around the mountain and after another hour opened into a small valley.

Slater took the lead. Carefully he made his way down a sloping, dusty trail toward a small adobe shack with a thin ribbon of smoke curling above the roof.

Madelina kicked her mount and followed.

71

The beekeeper was an old man with a salt-and-pepper beard. He squatted in front of his adobe shack, rocking on his heels. He wore white *peón* clothes and a big straw Chihuahua sombrero with a sugarloaf crown.

His eyes were sad.

Slater was asking him about his bees.

"*Sí*, amigo," he said to Slater, "the bees continue to be *muy malo*. And big? Do they grow big? *Madre de Dios*, as you can see they are now the size of eggs."

He pointed to three bees buzzing around a cactus blossom.

Madelina had to admit they were huge. Three of the biggest, strangest-looking bees she'd ever seen. They were black but speckled with bright yellow tufts. Moreover, as she listened carefully to the buzz, she realized that this was no quiet happy hum but a *zow-oooo! zow-oooo! zow-oooo!*

"You sure they're as vicious as ever?" Slater asked.

"*Sí*, amigo, and they grow worse daily. Last spring they swarmed my helper and killed him. He died of over a hundred stings. Since then I myself have been afraid to harvest the honey."

"If they're so dangerous, why do you raise them?"

"The man who sold me the first hive convinced me they could make twice as much honey as my other bees, and that they survived well in hot weather. They came from Africa, and he said they would adapt well to the climate."

"They apparently did."

"*Sí*, too well. They produce *mucho* honey but are so *muy maniaco*. I only desire to drive them away. But whenever I try, they come back. This small valley is the only decent country in a hundred miles of desert llano."

Slater gave him a wide grin. "How many hives of them African bees you got now?"

"Five, amigo."

"You think they'll fit on that old two-wheel oxcart you don't use no more?"

"*Si*, but—"

"No buts about it. Suppose I smoked them hives, knocked out the bees temporarily. While they be stunned, I load them five hives onto that cart, then haul them beyond that mountain where they could never find their way back?"

"But what would you do when the bees came to?"

"I'd have the cart lashed up tight as a gnat's asshole with them canvas shrouds I brung."

"Señor, that would be suicide. After suffering all that heat and captivity under the shroud, the bees would grow *muy* angry. They would no longer even be bees. Upon release, they would be fiends from hell. You would be signing your death warrant. I could not let you do it. When you released them, it would be suicide. I wouldn't wish them on my worst enemies. I wouldn't even wish them on those *muy bastardos* Comancheros who come here each month to rob, frighten, and harass."

"Too bad. That's where I was gonna take them. Through the old mine shaft with Bear Dog here pullin' your cart, right up to the edge of the shaft head. Then I was gonna cut the shrouds' thongs and push the wagon over the cliff face into the canyon."

It took a long moment for the enormity of Slater's plan to sink in.

A big smile slowly crossed the old man's face.

"*Sí*, senor, two hundred thousand swarming bees dropped right into that box canyon, right on top of them *muy bastardos* comancheros."

The old man's smile was immense.

"Let me get my smoke pot."

PART XVII

72

They stood at the mouth of the shaft, with Bear Dog harnessed to the oxcart. The stock was picketed near forage and water.

The old man had agreed to look after them if Slater and Madelina did not return.

Which looked like a serious possibility.

The bees were now recovering from their smoke inhalation and were fighting mad. This was no ordinary buzzing beneath the tarpaulin; this was a thunderous rumbling like the roar of a steam engine ready to blow its boilers.

"Señor, I trust that shroud has no tears or weak spots," Madelina asked. "When we get into that shaft there will be no escape. We could never get away from the bees if they got loose."

"We couldn't get away if they got out now," said Slater.

The answer seemed to pacify her.

However, it did nothing for Bear Dog. He was glaring back over his shoulder at Slater, his eyes narrowed to red slits. Not that he hadn't pulled big loads before. Hell, he'd pulled sleds laden with baled furs twice this heavy in the Yukon.

It was just that the sleds had never been loaded with killer bees and he'd never had to drag them into the maw of a pitch-black tunnel.

"Go on, now," Slater yelled at him. "Line 'em up. Move 'em on out. Mush."

Mush.

He'd actually said the Indian word.

Mush.

Meaning, pull the goddamn sled.

With a dreadful shudder, Bear Dog threw himself into the traces. Slater and the girl pushed the back of the growling, vibrating cart, and slowly the wheels began to move.

73

It was nearly 3:00 A.M. when they reached the shaft head, and now they stood there overlooking the Comanchero camp.

The thunderous rumbling in the cart had grown so raucous that they'd been forced to leave it in the shaft.

They were afraid the growling would rouse the camp.

Also Slater had work to do.

Taking the saddlebags off his shoulder, he opened them up.

They were filled with dynamite.

"You mean, amigo, we've been hauling dynamite all this way? From Norteamérica to Chihuahua?"

"It was harmless. The caps was the only thing that could set these sticks off, and I kept them wrapped in cotton in these here pouches in my other bags."

"But what do we need dynamite for when we have the bees?"

"There's only one way in and one way out of that box canyon. That's the pass. When those bees hit, them comancheros are gonna head for that pass like bats out of hell. Which is where these charges come in. There's a fault line, a deep thin seam running through the top of this cliff. If I can plant these charges there, I can bring down that cliff. We'll nail the sentries and them that's tryin' to escape in one fell swoop."

"Can you get up there?"

"This ledge goes straight to the top. No sweat. I'll be back before dawn. Then the fun begins."

74

Before Slater returned, Madelina could smell the smoke from the fuse.

The second he returned, he strapped Bear Dog back into the traces and yelled, "Mush!"

Bear Dog again threw himself into the apron and collar.

When they got the trembling, growling cart up to the shaft head, Slater cut Bear Dog out of the harness. With Madelina's help, he pushed, shoved, and worked the big cart wheels up to the very edge of the cliff face.

Now he unstrapped the Sharps "Big Fifty" from his back and slid the barrel tip down along the cliff face. He pulled the breech up under the bed of the cart.

He took his razor-sharp Arkansas toothpick out of his back sheath and handed it to Madelina.

"I'm leverin' this cart over the cliff. When it starts to go, you slash them ropes in the back and on the sides. And don't fall over."

He put his back into it. The cart began to rock, creak, and groan on its axles. It slid slowly over the precipice, and Madelina cut the ropes.

The cart went.

In some ways it seemed to Madelina a beautiful sight. As the cart slipped into the void, the sun was blazing bloodred over the rimrock, and the canvas shroud unfurled like a great gray topsail, flapping and waving in the breeze, all thirty feet of it.

During the nine-hundred-foot fall into the camp, the five hives separated and tumbled from the wagonbed.

And as each hive began its slow, cartwheeling descent, the bees came out.

These were no ordinary bees the way Madelina had always known them. They did not buzz playfully in small whirling clusters; they instantly swarmed into a dozen inky-black tornadoes, vast masses of pitchy balefire come to scourge the damned.

The noise escalated too. If before the oxcart had shaken with the awful rumble of *zow-eeee! zow-eeee! zow-eeee!* now the howling was horrendous—*zeeeeee! zeeeeee! zeeeeee!*—the piercing shrill of creatures gone insane with heat and captivity.

"Here," Slater said, handing Madelina his twelve-power sniper scope. "Maybe you'll see better."

But by then it was too late.

Their view of the canyon was totally obscured by the black swarms of screaming bees.

75

In one of the bucksaw brothel shacks, Sutherland, Judith McKillian, and Flynn had been drinking and debating, arguing whether it was safe to divide and spend some of the loot.

When the bees hit.

They looked out the hut's shuttered windows and, to their horror, saw that the sky was black with the apocalyptic swarms. The people outside were dying from hundreds of stings, dropping like flies, their bodies swelling grotesquely from the massive injection of venom.

Instantly they slammed the shutters shut.

"What happened?" Judith McKillian shouted.

"That fool of a beekeeper did it," Sutherland said.

"He wouldn't have the balls," Flynn said.

Sutherland and Flynn said it simultaneously: "Slater."

Suddenly McKillian pointed to the fireplace chimney.

It was vibrating.

Flynn's eyes were frantic. "You know the spring well? It's a thirty-foot drop. Make a run for it. But grab something to breathe with on the way. A handful of hollow reeds from the dried-up pond on the right. Go straight into the well. I'll release the windlass before I jump. We'll need the rope and bucket to climb out."

"If we survive," Sutherland said.

Flynn nodded. "Yes, if we survive."

Now the first bees were pouring out of the fireplace, their *zeeee! zeeee! zeeee!* earsplitting in the claustrophobic confines of the shack.

The three went charging out the door.

Into hell's abyss.

76

For a few seconds, the bees cleared in the middle of the camp. Madelina saw Flynn, Sutherland,

and the McKillian woman pile out of the shack. They were hit instantly.

A cloud of bees swept back over the center of the camp, and again all was obscured.

But by then Madelina had had enough.

During the brief parting of the bee swarms, Madelina had seen a whole lifetime of torture, including Sutherland's, Flynn's, and that of the McKillian woman. People everywhere were ballooned up to twice their normal size with the prodigious injections of venom. She'd watched them scream and thrash hysterically, their eyes wild with terror and despair, and then slowly, agonizingly, she'd watched them die.

Suddenly the side of the mountain blew.

The cliff stood three hundred yards to their right, and very simply, it turned into a sheet of red-orange flame. The top shook violently with an ear-cracking *ka-whomp! whomp! whomp!* The noise at that close range was deafening. The blast waves hit the rocks and the scrap around them, knocking down boulders and throwing gravel and scree in all directions.

The beams inside the tunnel trembled.

"Let's do it," Slater said, taking the scope from her. "The shaft is our only way off this cliff. If the blast has jarred loose any of the shoring timbers, we'll have to dig our way through. We better move it on out."

So be it. Madelina had had enough of her revenge. She'd seen the people who had done those terrible things to her and her family suffer a thousand times more horribly than she and her family had suffered.

She nodded her agreement.

And followed Slater and the dog down the shaft.

77

Flaco was checking on the sentries when he heard the bees hit.

Slater was his first conscious impression.

That and the sight of the oxcart and the five hives tumbling into the box canyon.

When the charges blew, he and the last two sentries felt the heat of the flash, even from nine hundred feet above the gorge.

When the shock waves hit, they were almost knocked off their feet.

Still, he and two of the sentries took off on foot, charging down the pass. Under a rainstorm of rocks, gravel, debris, and flying scree, the three of them ran.

And the world crashed down behind them.

78

The shock waves thundered through the shaft.
And took their toll.

Through every low, winding turn the shoring timbers buckled and groaned. Black choking dust coughed out of the walls and ceiling rock. Twice they'd found sections of the shaft collapsed, and they had had to stop, bolster the timberwork, dig out the fallen scree, and push on.

If the first trip through had taken five hours, the trip back took twice that.

If the growling bees had been nerve fraying, the fear of being buried in the collapsing tunnel was heart stopping.

During the last few hours their safety lamp died. They were trapped in gloom blacker than the pit.

It was then that Slater put his belt around Bear Dog's neck.

Madelina asked Slater in the Stygian gloom, "Do you really think he'll be able to see?"

"We're 'bout to find out."

Slowly, hesitantly, Bear Dog picked his way through the tunnel's rubble.

79

Flaco, Harv, and Packer stationed themselves in
the tunnel just outside the main stope, a mile
inside the entrance. Up ahead, they could hear
two people and the dog, banging and coughing.

They shielded a lighted pine knot behind a
blind turn and waited out of sight of the main
shaft, their guns cocked.

80

The three Comancheros had a good plan, but,
regrettably, no one had told them about the griz.

And the bear was definitely irate.

The old griz had been hibernating in his
winter lair deep in the shafts when he first
heard the ruckus.

Slater, Madelina, the dog, and what he swore was a howling horde of bees lumbered past his bolt hole.

And yet he did not move.

A hibernating griz is slow to rouse.

The blast, however, the falling timbers and choking dust, *that* had done it.

He rose from his lair and stumbled through the dust, smoke, and debris, heading for the main shaft.

81

When the griz entered the main tunnel, his eyes were shut tight against the dust, and he was sneezing convulsively.

Turning a blind corner, he lumbered smack into Flaco and his two friends.

Pandemonium reigned.

In the flash of the gunfire, it was obvious to the Comancheros that this was not Torn Slater.

This was a griz filled with rage at having been awakened from his winter's rest and at having several handgun rounds pumped into him at point-blank range.

The griz hit the three Comancheros like a fire-belching locomotive.

82

Bear Dog's muzzle may have been covered with dirt, and his nose may have been clogged bad.

But not that badly.

That was a grizzly.

Twice his leaders had caused him to do battle with these huge fiends, and twice was enough.

He broke from the belt leash and turned in his tracks.

He knocked Slater and Madelina ass-over-tea-kettle.

And made good his escape.

83

The last of the Comancheros' screams subsided.

There were no more sounds of men howling

and dying, or of the griz flinging them around the shaft like cordwood, or of the griz's own ear-cracking growls.

Now the only human survivors were Slater and the girl.

They waited in the gloom, the dog long gone behind them. They stared in rapt concentration at the far end of the big stope, where a blazing pine knot rolled across the floor, flickering erratically. Slater had his "Big Fifty" Sharps up at his shoulder, sighting it down the stope into the distant illumination.

Then they heard the noise. The soft slapping of grizzly pads. Coming toward them. The griz, silhouetted against the dying, sputtering torch, was moving uptunnel. For them. To finish them off, too.

Quietly, inaudibly, Slater shushed Madelina.

The flickering gloom deepened.

He had to wait until the last possible second.

Till the griz was on top of them.

In order to see him.

He could not squeeze off a round.

Not yet.

84

The thousand-pound griz with the long silver stripe down his back was halfway across the stope.

When the rifle discharged.

If before the handguns had angered him, the "Big Fifty" drove him berserk. The huge slug not only blazed across the top of the griz's shoulder, it whined off a wall and with a whistling *whap!* smacked him in the ass.

This wound was more than painful and terrifying.

It was humiliating.

So, when the big one with the knife in his teeth attacked, the enraged griz met him head-on, nailing him with a walloping right paw.

The man crashed into the left wall, and the knife dropped to the floor.

The griz bent over him, ignoring the frail girl. Taking one of the man's big shoulders in his jaws, he whirled him above his head, round and round.

Pausing periodically to slam him into a wall.

But as the griz worried his kill, Madelina saw the gleaming Arkansas toothpick. She snatched it up and, with a blood curdling whoop, vaulted the griz's back. Wrapping her legs around his throat, she drove the toothpick deep into his nape.

85

Up the tunnel, Bear Dog was slowly recovering from his panic.

True, he reasoned, he'd been badly mauled once before by the griz down in the pit.

But hadn't the leader saved him?

And wasn't this shaft right here a kind of pit?

Maybe this was all part of some strange game he'd never understood before.

And what if, in the middle of this game, he gave tail and ran?

What would his leader think of him?

And the girl?

And himself?

86

At the moment, Slater was not thinking of Bear Dog's betrayal.

He was staring up into the jumping, flickering glare of the blazing pine knot. He watched with swimming, wavering eyes as Madelina locked her legs around the grizzly's throat and repeatedly drove the Arkansas toothpick into his nape with both hands.

Weaponless and helpless, he watched the griz rise on his haunches, all thirteen feet of him, reach his paws over his head, and pluck her off his back like a small doll. Lifting her over his shoulder, he clutched her to his chest, stared into her sobbing, gasping face for a long, curious moment, the enfolded her in his murderous embrace.

In horror, Slater heard the sickening *crack!* of the girl's spine.

The griz threw her limp body into the wall and gazed at Slater. Still standing on his haunches and bending slightly at the waist, the griz threw back his massive head and roared.

Then Bear Dog hit him.

Slater could not believe his eyes. The dog hit his throat like a howitzer, clamping down on it like a vise, his hind paws clawing maniacally at the chest.

The griz exploded.

He locked Bear Dog in the same hellish hug he'd used on the girl.

But nothing happened.

The griz walked over to the nearest wall and slammed himself and the dog against the hard rock of the stope.

Repeatedly.

When that didn't work, and when Bear Dog's locked jaws cut through the jugular vein, like the griz in the pit, this one, too, pitched forward on top of him in an explosive floodtide of blood.

And died.

87

It took Slater an eternity to drag the dog one-armed out from under the griz.

Not that his efforts were appreciated.

Bear Dog had never whimpered before, and he wasn't whimpering now.

But he emitted soft, low-throated growls.

He might even have bitten Slater if he hadn't been half-paralyzed by his broken back.

Slater didn't care, though. He knew none of them had much time left. And what the hell, if they were going to die like this in the bowels of a collapsing mine stope, they ought to die together.

He did not want any of them to make the last trip alone.

He dragged Bear Dog over to the girl. He could see in the flickering light that she was still alive, but just barely.

Her eyes were vacant as the broken windows in an abandoned house.

He watched her sadly. It was clear that the death coming to her was not what she'd expected. Her face was violently contorted, and pain surged through her in hard, convulsive spasms. She choked on each breath, and her chest was detonating.

He thought he heard her whisper "Slater," but it could have been "padre" or it could have been water dripping in the shaft.

He could not tell.

In the darkness, she died.

88

Bear Dog was not pleased either. The pain was bad, but then pain was something he had endured all his life. He could accept that.

What he could not accept was dying.

Twice before he'd gazed on the naked face of death, and both times his leader had saved him. Once when he'd fought the griz in the pit, the other time when he'd fought the puma.

But when he looked up into his leader's face, he knew there was no hope.

His leader was dying too.

Somehow, that made him feel better. Always before he'd seen death as a damming up of his life's wild tide, and as such, he had hated it. But it did not seem that way this time. Rather, death was coming to him as a wall of white light.

Which he realized he must walk through.

Then his leader would walk through after him.

So you see, he said to himself, it won't be that bad. Beyond the light we'll be together, and who knows, perhaps we'll have quail to flush, bucks to pull down, track lines to run.

Together.

He turned his head up to Slater, to cheer him up, as if to say, "Come on, it'll be fun." His vision was wavering, but he made an enthusiastic attempt at a grin, and without even realizing that he did it, he stuck his muzzle into Slater's hand.

For the first time in his life, Bear Dog gave tongue.

Twice.

And died.

89

Slater leaned back against the stope. He held the dead girl propped up against the wall under his right arm. The dog's head lay still on his lap.

Unwittingly, he petted the dog.

Something he had never done.

What little strength he had left he focused on the dying pine-knot torch.

HELL HOUND

He knew that when the knot went out he would die in the dark and the dust.

But not alone.

He would die with his friends.

The torch was flickering, growing dim, and slowly Slater began to sing an old, old song:

Hush, little baby, don't you cry.
You know your daddy was born to die.
All my trials, Lord, soon be over.

PART XVIII

Don't look back, boy, on the trail back there
For the women that loved you or them that
    care.
There's a wailing train whistle, through your
    soul it's throbbed,
For the men that you killed and the trains that
    you robbed
For the banks that you hit and the women that
    sobbed.
It's followin' you up your trail.
Don't look back, boy, just listen to it wail.
Back in Yuma Jail.
—J.P. Paxton, "The Ballad of Outlaw Torn
    Slater," circa 1881

90

Calamity Jane Cannary sat at the green baize-covered poker table drinking a large glass of Old Crow. As soon as she downed it, she poured a second.

She couldn't help herself.

J.P. Paxton was singing his newest song.

She needed strength.

Rita and Candy joined her at the table, grinning. They loved the song, damn them.

But then, everybody loved it.

It was a nationwide success.

Calamity tried to blot out the wretched lyrics, but still they came through.

The Comancheros staked you out
On the bottom of the canyon floor.
On a rack of fire, a convulsive cross,
They skinned you to your gore.
They racked you to your soul.
They broke you on the wheel.
They scorched you to your balls.
Your hellish fate they sealed.

HELL HOUND

But your tortured life you haven't lost
Though your soul was never found.
On a twisted cross of fiery death
You were saved by a coal-black hound.
A hound that slaughters the massive griz
And sleeps in the devil's lair.
A hound that beds down puma cats,
You best beware of the Bear.

For Bear Dog ain't no friend to man
For a mutt's life he don't care.
Give him trail, just let him pass,
You best beware of the Bear.

A Christian family took you in,
Gave you a home and bed.
They nursed you through that bloody hell
Though your warrant reads, "Wanted: Dead."
And them Comancheros don't forget.
That family'll never escape.
The family men they will hang and shoot,
The daughter repeatedly rape.

So when the daughter tracks you down,
Those bills are already due.
You'll find the ones that done her wrong,
You, the girl, that hell-bent hound.
They'll curse the day they're born,
Their mothers for giving them birth.
You'll track those bastards one by one
Though they flee to the ends of the earth.

With that dog who ain't no friend to man
Who sleeps in the devil's lair.
The dog who beds down puma cats,
You best beware of the Bear.

They'll curse the day they're born,
Their mothers for giving them birth.
You'll track those bastards one by one
Though they flee to the ends of the earth.
You, the girl, that hell-bent hound,
You're hell's own spawn, I swear.
Them Comancheros are better off dead.
They best beware of the Bear.

The crowd stamped and clapped enthusiastically.

They could enjoy it, thought Calamity.

Their man wasn't leaving them today.

They weren't the ones who had to go after him on that last venture.

They didn't have to dig him out of that collapsing mine shaft more dead than alive.

They didn't have to stitch him back together, splint the bones, and haul him halfway across Chihuahua dodging *federales* and then gringo lawmen every step of the way.

They hadn't seen the inside of the Comanchero camp where she and the Professor had gone to look for him. They hadn't had to gaze on those hundreds of thousands of dead bees covering the camp like a dense, dried-up crust. The bodies of the victims were stung hundreds, even thousands, of times, their faces bloated and misshapen far beyond any similarity to humankind.

And worst of all, when she'd looked down in that well.

There were more bees.

Thousands of the killers.

Still alive.

They were roosting on the bucket rope, the top edge of the old wooden bucket, and along the sides of the well.

And the three bodies in the water. She'd never seen anything like it. They had hollow reeds still clenched in their teeth, still sticking straight up out of the water.

They were terribly swollen from all the bites they'd sustained.

They were obviously dead.

They had to be.

But, now that she thought about it, that's what bothered her. Why were those reeds sticking straight up, and why did the three of them seem to be staring at the bees?

If they were dead.

All Calamity knew was that she did not care. When she had seen those live bees, she and the Professor had hauled ass and not looked back.

She tossed off another shot.

She was still not looking back.

91

Calamity glanced over her shoulder at the big man lumbering down the stairs. He had saddle-bags tossed over his shoulders, guns shoved into his pants, and his new Stetson fixed firmly on his head.

Outlaw Torn Slater was on the road.

He stopped by the table. "I'm leavin' now, but I'll be back."

Calamity shrugged. The girls got up and kissed his cheek, then left them alone for whatever little privacy there was in a border-town brothel.

"Don't suppose you'd care to tell me where or why you're goin'?"

"You wouldn't believe me if I did."

"Try me."

"To Chihuahua to see a whore."

"Hell, we got lots of them around here. Hired two more last night. What's so special 'bout Chihuahua?"

For the first time in all the years Clem had known Slater, he looked embarrassed.

"I'm gonna reform her."

"Don't sound like your kind of work."

"It is now."

Clem looked astonished.

Slater glanced around the room nervously. He studied Princess for a moment. A recent mother, she now had a litter of pups, which were feeding hungrily.

Except for one.

With her left paw she was batting away a huge black pup.

"What's the matter over there?" Slater asked.

Clem smiled. "Oh, that damn pup? The big black one? He keeps beatin' up on the rest of them. She can't even let him feed 'cause he's always scarin' the others away. He also bites the shit out of me and anyone else tries to get near him. I asked one of the stableboys to drown the fucker. Guess he ain't got around to it yet."

Slater gave Clem a long look.

"Get the hell out of here," she said.

He wheeled around and headed for the batwing doors. Just before he hit them, to her surprise, she saw him bend at the waist. In one fluid motion, he swept up the ferocious black pup, slung him over his shoulder, and hit the doors.

That was her last image of Outlaw Torn Slater.

Passing through the swinging doors.

The big black pup on his shoulders, yelping, whining, and whimpering.

Then nuzzling the back of Slater's neck.

SPECIAL PREVIEW

Here are some exciting scenes from

Devil's Sting

the next scorching adventure
in the Torn Slater series!

1

A tall man stood on the black wrought-iron balcony overlooking the main street of El Carrizo. His tan, sweat-stained plainsman's hat was slanted low over his eyes, shading them from the searing desert sun. His Levi's and collarless brown shirt were still dusty after the long ride from Chihuahua. The saddleless dun, tied to the hitchrack below, looked cooked up and broken down.

His fine Appaloosa and his girl's roan were stalled at the stable up the street. They were enjoying rest and feed. The dun was either wind-broken or down with the contagion. The man would make up his mind which in a few more hours. If it was the former and not too serious, the man would sell or trade him to a kindly-looking *peón*. If it was the latter, he would take him into the llano, give him a few kind words, and put him down.

The man glanced up and down the dusty street. A scattering of two dozen adobe shacks baked in the fierce desert heat. The sun was at its zenith, and the few observable *peónes* had already begun their afternoon siesta in the shade of their hovels and jacales. Otherwise, nothing. No rising smoke, no breath of breeze, no horses or dogs or even the usual assortment of random chickens pecking up the road.

For the moment, El Carrizo was dead.

But only for the moment. El Carrizo was a Mejicano hurrah town, a south-of-the-border sink of iniquity waiting for sundown. El Carrizo seemed to exist solely as a stopping-off point, a limbo for wrongdoers and desperadoes, for men on the slippery slope to the infernal pit. In El Carrizo they paused long enough to *chinga* some *putas,* belt back the local mescal, and enjoy a hand of cards.

Then, like diamondbacks at nightfall, they spat their foul poison and were gone.

The man up on the balcony squinted his flat black eyes, as if expecting something or someone to disturb the town's dead-hot calm. As he did, the corners split and cracked into a sun-darkened maze of deeply etched, alkalai-streaked lines.

The hard inheritance of too many years in the arid border country.

Slowly, the man turned on his heel and headed back into the hotel room.

2

He had the best room in the hotel. The thick adobe made it cool in the day and comfortable at night. It had a big feather tick, a wall coat rack, and two bentwood chairs from the bar.

By El Carrizo standards he was in the Presidential Suite of the Mark Hopkins.

But the man was not concerned with these furnishings. Instead, his gaze fell on the petite young thing flung across the bed, her lissome body twisted under the thin sheet in a tautly outlined, astonishingly sensual S-curve. Her eyes were closed, and her chest rose and fell so deeply and rhythmically that she looked as if she could sleep her way through Antietam.

She yawned and stretched. The slight movement gently tossed a dozen strands of her waist-length raven hair across her left cheek. Several fell casually across the girl's wet, parted lips.

Remembering what she had done with those pouty bee-stung lips less than an hour ago made the man's groin ache.

He turned his gaze to the petulant woman sitting in the bentwood chair to his right. Like himself, she was dressed in trail garb—Levi's, a collarless tan shirt, a big cross-drawn Colt, roweled boots, and a black Stetson, the band studded with conchos—all of it stained with sweat and dust. She had reddish-brown hair pulled back into a tight ponytail, good bones, and, the man knew, under the bulky clothes she had a strong, shapely body. Long of leg. High of breast. Firm of bottom. And, unlike his own flat, expressionless, coal-black stare, her eyes promised merriment, good times, and, if you were man enough, better ones to come.

But not now.

They had spent the better part of an hour fighting. And after one more look into those blazing brown orbs, he knew she was not done.

Slowly, Torn Slater began to massage his temples. The meeting—which *she* had demanded and arranged—here in El Carrizo had begun badly. She had walked in on him just as he was putting the blocks to that luscious young thing, who at that moment had been groaning and writhing on the tick. Slater thought with a grin that it could have piqued Calamity's jealousy.

Even so, Slater's motives had been laudable. He had traveled to Mejico to liberate this young puta from a stone-cold, dog-mean pimp. That done, he was to transport her across the North American border. Up there, the only two decent law-abiding people the outlaw knew would see that she was properly looked after.

Now that she was safely out of the pimp's reach.

Unfortunately, nothing is ever as simple as it seems.

The dog-mean pimp turned out also to be a snake-mean bandido.

And his pursuit was relentless.

It was now clear that Rozanna would never be safe from Aquilar and his four men—never.

Until Torn Slater killed them.

In El Carrizo he was determined to make his stand.

3

Slowly, Calamity Jane Cannary stood up. "I got the word on that boy what's on your backtrail.

He's nothin' but hair, rattles, and diamondback venom. 'Fore your bitch passed out, she claimed he once ate a raw vulture and washed it down with puma piss."

"You don't like my plan none?"

"You call that a plan? Takin' on five owlhooters with one shitty belt gun?"

"It do skate like thin ice, don't it?" Slater said solemnly.

"Thinner'n cow piss on a flat fuckin' rock."

"Ain't nothin' I can say to make it any better."

"You could reconsider Sutherland's offer."

"Clem—"

"Now don't 'Clem' me. Sutherland's been in the ground five months, but 'fore he went he found his God. And he changed his will. And we're in it."

"Clem—"

"Now, damn you, Torn Slater, it's bound to be worth a mint. All we gotta do to collect it is be at the readin'. It's down in that old Sonora monastery in the Sierras. You even been granted immunity. Them Philadelphia lawyers of his promised. It's goddamn foolproof."

"It ain't me. I never liked Sutherland. I even scalped him once. And hung him by the hocks over a slow-burnin' fire."

"Yeah? Then answer me this: Sutherland, he died rich and famous. His name was blazoned in newspaper headlines all over the West. And you? How'll you go? You'll die broke and alone, boot-buried in some wind-scoured boneyard, lucky to have a scrapwood casket or get wrapped up in an old horse hide. Sutherland owned *countries*, and the only real estate you'll ever have is that six-foot hole they plant you in. No kids to sob, no wife to mourn your passin'. You'll die unknown in a pauper's grave. There won't be nobody there to care or to pull the grass up over your head." Calamity thumped her chest hard. "The same here. The same for me."

"That may be, but I ain't got no truck with Sutherland."

"You tellin' me you wouldn't take his cash?" Calamity asked, unbelieving.

"Sure I would. With his nuts in my fist and my red-hot smokin' Colt in his mouth. I'd *take* it from him. But I wouldn't go suckin' 'round after it."

"Bill Cody'll be there. Sitting Bull. Belle Starr. Me. Geronimo. Buntline. All of us what Sutherland thought he wronged. It's okay for us to get rich, but not you. You too good for the money or something?"

"It ain't me. It ain't what I am. And it sure as shit ain't what I do."

4

Slater was finishing packing his gear when Rozanna woke. She brushed the long raven hair out of her mouth and yawned. Calamity looked her up and down disdainfully.

"She any good?" Clem asked Slater.

"Like gettin' head from a hydrophobic bat."

"I also fucked his brains out," Rozanna added.

"Obviously," Calamity rasped.

"You two weren't fighting?" Rozanna asked. "I thought I heard you call him *el stupido*."

Clem looked at Slater appraisingly. "Him stupid? Hell, he has to tie a string to his dick so he can find it. Has to tie it to the shithouse door so he can find his way out."

"It were the war that done it to me," Slater said dryly.

Clem shook her head derisively. "I heard it was all them years in jail. Heard some prison doctor amputated your brain and replaced it with road apples. Was he the one what give you them enemas with a hydraulic hose?"

"Naw," Slater grinned, "the generals done that one. At Shiloh. That's why I joined up with Quantrill."

Rozanna stared at him quizzically, unsure about the gringo humor. She looked back at Calamity. "Is he really so *stupido*?"

"Honey, you tell me What's the story on them boyfriends of yours? Heard they got hands strong enough to straighten cold horseshoes. And rough enough to hammer fence posts into hard ground. Hear them five's mean enough to kill rocks. Well, this ol' boy is takin' on all of them with one pissy belt gun."

Rozanna fixed Slater with a tight stare. "Amigo, that is not very smart. Do you use that gun well?"

"Naw," Calamity answered, "he don't use it at

all. He just shouts magic chants at 'em and makes himself invisible."

Slater threw his saddlebags over his shoulder and headed toward the door.

"Señor," Rozanna asked, "is that all you have? That one gun?"

"'Fraid so."

"You will need more than that. Much more."

Slater looked at Calamity and smiled. A long, slow smile. A smile to melt the hardest whore's heart.

Or turn an honest woman bad.

"I'd bring my Gatling but it stretches the holster."

He pushed open the door and headed for the stairs.

5

Time.

The wait seemed to take forever, but Slater was used to that.

Time.

Time was when you were captured by Apaches at the age of twelve and by the age of fifteen were leading raiding parties.

Time.

Time was leading the last charge at Shiloh, while ten thousand screaming Yankees shot your comrades to pieces. Time was turning away the overhanded thrust of a Yankee bayonet, blunting the attack with an elbow, and after putting a knee to the Yankee's crotch, breaking his wrist. Time was forcing him face-down into the Shiloh mud, shoving a knee into his back, grabbing him by the throat and chin, and wrenching hard on his head till, audible above the din of cannons and musket, you heard the dull *crack!* of the breaking neck. Time was crawling back through the mud and muck and bursting shells to your own rebel trench, leaving the dead Yankee lying in a pool of your own blood.

Time.

Time was the years with Quantrill and Bloody Bill, looting and burning and above all murdering your way through Bloody Kansas and Bloodier Missouri. Time was riding with Frank and Jess and Coleman Younger after the war, sticking to banks and trains to vent your rage.

Time.

Time was the long years spent on the owlhoot trail and the longer ones spent in Yuma and Sonora Prisons. In shackles and leg irons. On the long road doing hard time. Time. Time was spent chained to the flogging post or locked in the hot box or buried at the bottom of Diaz's slave-labor mines in the hideous Sulphur Shaft.

Time.

Time was having friends like Frank and Jess and Coleman Younger and Bill Hickok and Marquez and the old doc. Time was looking down your backtrail and knowing that they were in jail or in the grave and there was nothing you could do to alter these things or even to help.

Time.

Time was sitting at an empty cantina table, and on it, a big tricked-out Spanish saddle full of inlaid silver and turquoise and ebony leather. Time was carefully rubbing neat's-foot oil into the cantle and the leathers, making it look shiny and smooth, expensive and new for the five guests who would soon be walking through the front door.

With their guns.

Time.

Time was waiting.

Waiting without dread or hope or even fear.

Time.

And where it would end, God only knew.

6

Up the room, Clem sat with the Winchester straddling her knees.

"What do you think of Señor Slater?" Calamity asked Rozanna.

"When I think of him, I hurt *muy malo*."

"In your heart?"

"In my crotch."

"I don't know as I like that," Calamity said ruefully.

"So? Señor Slater, he no care you fuck all your men."

Calamity shrugged. "He says men like him and Bill Hickok, they don't care."

"You say this Hickok, he fuck you too? And he no care?"

"Yes."

"Where's he now?"

"He's dead."

Rozanna nodded knowingly. "*Sí, es verdad.* He no care."

"It weren't like that."

"No? What was it like? When he made love to you."

"Oh, it weren't much. Back archin' like a bent bow, crotch exploding with molten magma. If you get what I mean. Jaw gaped, head lolling and rolling back and forth over the edge of the bed, or, if it were out on the trail, maybe over the saddle. Throat sobbing, breath gasping. It weren't nothin' special."

"And Slater, he no get jealous?"

"Only over pesos."

"That is good. When I go back to my profession, I would not want him angry at my *hombres.*"

"Mean you ain't got no plans for reformin'?"

"After Señor Slater? *Madre mia!* I could be the *grande puta* of El Presidente Diaz. *Ey!* The things that man has shown me! They would be worth a fortune in Mejico City."

"Yeah," Calamity agreed. "When I walked in here, it didn't look like Sunday-Go-to-Meetin'. Half-expected firestorms, rock slides, and eruptin' volcanoes."

"He is *muy hombre!*" Rozanna exclaimed.

"What the hell did your sister think you was?

Something he could change from brothel whore to fairy-tale princess with a kiss?"

"Bless her sacred soul, she was not practical."

"Does Slater know all this?"

"Not yet. I did not wish to hurt his feelings."

"Then maybe it's time to pull his coat."

She stood and started toward the door.

Then came to an abrupt stop.

Standing in the door was the biggest, meanest bandido she'd ever seen, nothing but teeth, beard, and crisscrossed bandoleers.

"Hi, *bebé*," Aquilar said to Rozanna. "Long time no see."

The gun leveled at Calamity's gut was Slater's navy Colt.